A King Production presents…

Baller Bitches
VOLUME 2

A NOVEL
JOY DEJA KING

ISBN 13: 978-0986004551

ISBN 10: 0986004553
Cover concept by Joy Deja King
Cover layout and graphic design by www.MarionDesigns.com
Typesetting: Keith Saunders
Editors: Linda Williams

Library of Congress Cataloging-in-Publication Data;
A King Production
Baller Bitches Volume 2: a series/by Joy Deja King
For complete Library of Congress Copyright info visit;
www.joydejaking.com

A KING PRODUCTION

A King Production
P.O. Box 912, Collierville, TN 38027

Dedication

This Book is Dedicated To My:
Family, Readers and Supporters.
I LOVE you guys so much. Please believe that!!

A KING PRODUCTION

Baller Bitches

VOLUME 2
PARTS 4-6

A NOVEL

JOY DEJA KING

Diamond

Where the fuck am I? And what the fuck happened? Those questions were ringing in my head as I began coming out of what felt like the darkest nightmare of my life. My head was throbbing and my mouth felt dry. I hadn't felt this fucked up since I was head butted with that gun when I was robbed. I tried to raise my body up, but it was as if I was lurking into darkness. I quickly realized it was because my eyes were still shut, for some reason I couldn't seem to open them. I felt this pressure keeping them glued closed but when I swung my arms against my eyes I felt nothing.

"I'm losing my fuckin' mind," I mumbled before slowly laying back down. I took a deep breath and decided I would start from scratch and try this again. Right when I was about to massage my temples, hoping it would help relieve the awful pain I was in which would then allow me to open my fuckin' eyes, I heard a door open and a voice speak to me.

"Diamond, can you hear me?"

"Yes, who are you and where am I?"

"Open your eyes."

"I'm trying, but my head feels like it's about to explode and every time I try to open my eyes they flicker shut," I complained as I rubbed the back of my head and felt a semi large bump. "What the fuck is going on! How did I get this knot on my head?" I shouted, feeling as if I was on the verge of having a nervous break down.

"Calm down," the voice said, not seeming the least bit rattled by my on edge behavior. I heard something open and close then a few seconds later I felt a cold bottle being placed in my hand.

"What's this?"

"Bottled water and take two of these. It will help you relax." For some reason even though I couldn't see their face and I had no idea who I was listening to, I did what the person said without hesitation. Even in my daze, something about the person seemed familiar and safe.

"What happened and where am I?"

"Lay back and chill. Give the medicine a little time to kick in and hopefully things will start coming back to you. I'll be back in about thirty minutes."

I wanted to scream out that I didn't want the person to leave but the comfort of laying back and resting my head won out. I knew I had to calm down. Although my excruciating headache was playing a major part I also believed extreme anxiety was another reason I couldn't seem to open my eyes all the way. Instead of going with my initial desire to scream at the top of my lungs, I started visualizing myself lying on the beach on top of Cameron with the sand underneath our bodies and the cool waves hitting our skin. We were at peace, something I hadn't felt in what seemed like forever. As I let my mind travel to a moment of serenity, the throbbing seemed to begin to subside.

As I dozed off thinking about frolicking on a beach with Cameron, my wishful thinking dream quickly turned into a realistic nightmare. Flashbacks began randomly popping in my head but they seemed to be out of sequence. At first I thought again my mind was playing tricks on me and I was imagining some shit that never happened, but it all seemed too real. I wanted to make it stop but it wouldn't. I felt like I was fighting for my life.

"Somebody help me!" I yelled out over and over again until I finally felt someone standing over me. "I can see," I said rising up like a mummy with my eyes wide open.

Kennedy

After Cameron called me I turned on the news and saw the coverage of Diamond's death. The reporter was standing in front of the blocked off crime scene, but I recognized Diamond's bullet ridden Escalade in the back because of the dark tinted windows and custom rims. I wanted to turn off the television, believing if I stopped watching that none of this would be true, but I couldn't turn away from the screen. I listened as the reporter talked about Diamond being out on bail on drug related charges and that they were speculating the shooting might be some sort of retaliation. Of course every other sentence that came out of the reporter's mouth mentioned that Diamond was the girlfriend of NBA superstar Cameron Robinson. That was the sole reason this story was breaking news.

"Pick up the fuckin' phone!" I screamed as I kept redialing Blair's number. She hadn't answered her phone since my initial call telling her Diamond was dead. After I told her there was nothing but silence and then the call hung up. So, not only was I devastated about Diamond I was stressing about Blair. When I felt my phone vibrating in my hand, I instantly looked down hoping I would see Blair's name flashing across my screen, but it wasn't, it was some number I didn't recognize. I decided to answer hoping it was some information about Diamond's death or Blair's whereabouts.

"Hello."

"Where is Blair?" I immediately wanted to hit end when I heard the deep toned arrogant voice on the other end of my phone. "Answer my question," he demanded.

"Who is this?" I asked although I knew exactly who it was. I wanted him to clearly hear the annoyance dripping from my voice.

"This is Michael Frost."

"How did you get my phone number? Oh, let me guess...does Darcy know you wanted my number so you could track down your ex?" I asked in my most condescending voice.

"Just answer my question. Where is Blair?"

"Listen, unlike some other people in your life, when you say jump I don't say how high. But I don't know where Blair is and even if I did, I wouldn't tell you."

"So you want me to believe that you had nothing to do with her walking the red carpet tonight with Skee Patron?"

"You really need to seek help for your stalker tendencies."

"Stop the bullshit games, Kennedy. I know it's you setting Blair up on these dates trying to give her nonexistent career a boost. But you're close to ruining the best thing that ever happened to her...me."

"Michael, you picked the wrong night for this shit!

I'm not in the mood to listen to you suck your own dick. I don't know where Blair is and please lose my fuckin' number!" After I ended the call Michael had the nerves to keep calling me back for the next fifteen minutes. "This fuck is such a psycho!" I belted tossing my phone down on the couch.

Blair

I slowly opened my eyes, awakening from my sleep. My first thought was the smoothness of the silk sheets beneath my body as I glided across the bed. Then instantly I stared down noticing my bra and panty clad body. I grabbed the quilt and pulled it tightly against my chest. As I looked around getting a clear view of my surroundings I felt completely naked. The bedroom area was open to an atrium, sharing the light and allowing for views out in all directions. There was a draped entry and the all white decor did highlight the rich charcoal-grey, what looked to be eucalyptus floors. I noticed a stone backdrop to the bed that seemed to unite the finishes on some of the other stone accents throughout the apartment that I could see from where I was positioned.

There were countless days that I spent hours going through design magazines learning the different specs of luxury homes and apartments. I imagined being able to afford to live in one of those places in the future, so to wake up in a crib, that seemed to be ripped right out of one of the pages in the magazine, had my mind spinning. Right when I was about to ask myself whose ridiculous sick crib I was in, I instantly recalled my night with Skee Patron.

"Good morning, beautiful," Skee said, interrupting all the thoughts that were about to run through my mind.

"How did I end up in your bed...did we have sex?" the question slipped from my tongue without thinking. I felt stupid for asking, but I wanted to know.

Skee gave me a slight smile before responding. "You don't remember what happened last night?"

"Bits and pieces. It's all still a little sketchy. But I woke up in my bra and panties so of course I had to ask."

"Those Molly's really did a number on you. But give yourself a little time. Everything will start coming back to you. But to answer your question, if we had sex, if we had, you wouldn't have woken up in your bra and panties, you would be naked."

I felt relieved that we didn't have sex but I also felt embarrassed that I was having trouble with what went down between us. I remembered walking in the party with Skee and feeling like a superstar, then popping the Molly's with Skee and feeling extremely free...too free. *Oh shit! I saw Kirk and he saw me making out with Skee. Fuck! What else happened* I thought to myself as my memories of last night quickly started coming back to haunt me.

"If we didn't have sex why did I come back here to your place?" Although I was remembering a lot, there were still some fuzzy blank areas that I needed Skee to fill in for me.

"We were in the car and yes my driver was headed back to my place so we could further enjoy each other's company, but you passed out. I couldn't remember where you lived so I brought you back here, took off your clothes and put you in bed. I didn't even sleep in here with you. I stayed in one of the guest bedrooms."

"I appreciate that."

"I've never had sex with a woman unless it was consensual and even as good as you looked last night, that tradition wasn't going to change."

"Point taken. But back to what happened in the car. One moment I was alert and the next I just passed out?"

"Basically. We were talking, you got a phone call and then you were out cold. But you did have a couple of Molly's. It might've been too much for your first time. I mean..."

"Wait a minute," I said cutting Skee off. "A phone call." My eyes widened and a rush of despair flooded me. "Where's my phone?" I asked trying not to become hysterical as the call I received right before I passed out replayed in my mind. I was praying that the Molly had my head so screwed up that what I thought I heard was simply a figment of my imagination.

"Hold on a second. I put it in your purse. I'll go get it." When Skee walked out I felt tears swelling up in my eyes. A sharp pain was pounding in my heart and I felt as if I was about to pass out for a second time.

"Is everything ok?" he asked with what sounded like authentic concern. I practically yanked my purse out of Skee's hand.

"I won't know until after I make this phone call," I said, before calling Kennedy. It seemed like my heartbeat was getting louder and louder with each ring until finally Kennedy answered her phone.

Diamond

"Renny, you're the one who brought me here?" I questioned when I opened my eyes and he was standing beside the bed.

"Yeah, I brought you here. I'm glad you can open your eyes now but you still don't remember anything?"

"Right before I opened my eyes I had these images of me being in a car arguing with some girl, then shit got crazy and I felt something hit me in the back of the head. I don't know if I was having a bad nightmare, but something about it seemed so real."

"That's because it was real."

"Huh...wait that really happened?"

"I wasn't there for that part, but from what I pieced together once I did get there that sounds about right."

"Wait, I know what happened," I said, sitting straight up. This nervous excitement shot through me as the idea of being able to tell my story was within reach.

"Tell me what you remember," Renny said, taking a seat.

"Give me a second. I'm trying to clear up a couple

things in my mind before I start."

"Take your time." Renny's patience and the calmness he exuded were allowing me to really process everything I was remembering.

"Oh my fuckin' goodness I was set up! That bitch set me up!"

"Who set you up?"

"I got a phone call around six o'clock yesterday from this girl named Tisha that I knew from the neighborhood. We weren't friends but we were cool."

"When she called you, what did she say?"

"She told me she had some information about Parish but she didn't want to discuss it over the phone."

"How did she know Parish?"

"That's what I asked her, but she told me she didn't know Parish. She said one of her girlfriends used to fuck with him but they broke up after she caught him cheating and he turned around and beat her ass for catching him. Tisha went on to tell me that a few days ago she and her friend were at her apartment just talking and her friend started talking shit about Parish. Tisha told me that what her friend said shook her up and she had to tell me because it could possibly save my life and keep me out of jail. But it was all a set up so I would meet her."

"What happened when you met up with her?"

"When I pulled up next to her, she told me to get into her car so we could talk and I did. At first Tisha seemed cool. She started going over the conversation she had with her friend again and I listened but then she flipped. She said I fucked up going after Parish and I was a dead bitch. After she said that I started thinking about these crank calls I had been getting with somebody saying I was a dead bitch. Right when I was about to lounge at her with my fist, I felt a sharp pain in the back of my head and I don't remember anything after that until I woke up here."

"I'm glad you were able to fill in some missing information for me," Renny said, as if in deep thought.

"Well maybe now you can return the favor because I need to know how I went from being inside Tisha's car to being here in this bed."

"As you know I was working on eliminating both Parish and Tech so I had my people keeping tabs on both of them. Last night I got a disturbing call from my workers who were handling the job saying they got word that your life was in danger and it might be too late."

"Are you serious!" I started shaking my head realizing that instead of sitting here complaining about a knot on the back of my head, my mom could've been making my funeral arrangements.

"I told them if you ended up dead then they might as well kill themselves too because you dying wasn't an option."

"You had my back like that?"

"You came to me for help. If something would've happened to you, I would've felt responsible."

"The only person responsible for this bullshit going on in my life right now is Parish."

"Hopefully he won't be a problem much longer."

"Clearly your workers were able to save me but

how?"

"They made it just in time. When they pulled up you were knocked out being carried to your Escalade."

"Why were they taking me back to my car?"

"From what my workers told me. The plan was while you were out cold they would place your body behind the wheel. Plant some drugs and then leave. Once they were gone another guy would come and shoot up your truck and kill you in the process."

"They wanted it to look like a drug deal gone bad," I said shaking my head in disgust.

"Exactly. But my workers sneaked up behind them and by the time they realized what was happening their life was already over."

"Who was the other person?"

"I have no idea, just some girl. Neither one of them had ID just their phones. That's why I liked the fact you could give me at least one of their names. With that information my people will be able to find out who the other girl was."

"I'm sure Parish knows by now I'm still alive so I'm sure he's plotting his next hit."

"We bought ourselves some time to throw him off for a lil' bit."

"What do mean? How did you do that?" I asked, totally confused.

"After they killed both girls, they placed one of them behind the wheel where you were supposed to be and put the other one in the trunk of the car and drove off, while the other worker brought you to me."

"So they think it was me in the car they killed?"

"Yep. The girl's cell phones came in handy. Because the guy sent a text asking was it a go and after everything was in place my worker replied with a simple yes. And soon after the dude showed up and sprayed your truck up."

"Unfuckin' believable."

"Speaking of phones let me get mine. I need to call Cameron. I'm sure he's worried about me."

"We don't have it. They said it must've been left in your car."

"That must mean my purse is in the car too."

"Yep."

"Do you think the cops found the body yet?"

"Based on the location your car was at, definitely."

"If *my* purse was left in *my* car and the girl didn't have any ID on her, they probably think the dead body is me. And at first glance based on my driver's license photo we could easily pass for being the same person. Fuck! Fuck! Fuck! Fuck! I have to call Cameron and my mother. What if the police called my mother and told her I was dead. She's gonna have a freakin' heart attack," I ranted, as I hopped out the bed determined to get to a phone. *Diamond, calm down and get back in the bed. You took a serious hit to your head. You need to lie down* I said to myself, trying to listen to my voice of reason. "Fine, then bring a phone to me."

"Listen, let's wait a minute. That's actually good news."

"How is that good news for Cameron or God forbid my mother to think I'm dead!"

"Because it gives us more time to eliminate Parish

and whoever else wants to kill you. If they think you're already dead then it will be easier for us to catch them with their guard down. Another one of my workers is already on it. He followed the shooter that lit up your truck and Parish 'bout to be taken care of too."

"Are you sure?"

"Positive. You're alive aren't you? I got this. All I needed was a little extra time and now that we know about the purse we have even more."

"But what about my mother?"

"The bad news is the police probably have called her to come identify the body. The good news is when she gets there she'll realize it's not you. Hopefully by then, everything is handled on our end and it will be safe for you to go home to your man."

"I hate to put my mother through that, but I'm sure she rather me not be dead but instead very much alive."

Kennedy

"Blair, where the hell have you been!" I shouted into the phone. "I've been worried sick about you! This is the wrong time for you to get missing!"

"I apologize but we can discuss that later. Just please tell me I didn't hear what I think I heard you say last night." I heard Blair's voice cracking although I could tell she was trying to restrain herself.

"You did hear what I said correctly," I countered, not wanting to say it out loud. I too was trying to keep my emotions in check but I couldn't. I burst into tears before I could say another word.

"NOOOOOOOO! This can't be true," Blair cried out, as what I said sunk in. "Diamond can't be dead she just can't!" Blair was now hysterical and at the moment I wished so bad that wherever she was I was right there with her so we could cry together.

I kept calling out to Blair wanting to calm her down but she ignored my pleas. Just like last night the phone went dead and I still didn't know where the hell she was. I decided to call her back but she wouldn't answer. Blair and Diamond basically grew up together and that was her best friend so I knew she was taking it super hard.

"I can't sit around here worrying about Blair. I want to be able to mourn and cry with somebody that understands what I'm going through and right now Blair is not available," I said out loud as I was walking towards the bathroom to take a shower. "I know what I can do," I said, continuing with my seething. "I'll go see Diamond's mother. That's what I'll do. I'm sure she needs a shoulder to cry on, probably more than me."

I rushed to the bathroom anxious to shower and get ready, so I could go see Diamond's mom. I figured she was distraught and now we could mourn together. After I thought about that another round of an even deeper depression hit me. What about Destiny I thought. She loved Diamond so much and now her mother is gone. *How will Destiny get by? Who will explain to her what happened to her mother? Will Destiny get to stay with her grandmother or will Rico get custody?* I had so many questions running around my brain and all I wanted was answers.

When I got to Diamond's mother's house, I stayed out front for about fifteen minutes before I knocked on the door. I had to work myself up to see her. I was tempted to turn around and not see her at all but I decided not to be a chump.

Knock....Knock...Knock

It felt like it took forever for someone to open the door. *Maybe this is a sign that I'm supposed to bolt* I thought, as I was once again tempted to walk away until I heard the door open.

"Ms. O'Toole, how are you?" I felt like an idiot asking the question as soon as it left my mouth. Her eyes were red and swollen, clearly from crying but my nervousness had gotten the best of me.

"I've been better," she answered solemnly. "Please come in."

"Thanks so much for inviting me in. I'm sure you don't really want to be bothered with anyone right now."

"Honestly I could use the company. Can I get you something?"

"No, I'm fine," I said, before sitting down on the sofa.

"I still can't believe my baby is gone. If it wasn't for Destiny I don't think I would be able to go on. But I know my grandbaby needs me."

"Where is Destiny?"

"With her daddy. I'm glad she spent the night with him 'cause if she had been here when I got the news I would've scared the poor child from all my hollering."

"I could only imagine. I'm still having a hard time wrapping my head around it. Have you found out anymore information about what happened?"

"Hell No! When the police called me they were so vague. I got more info from watching the news. I'm supposed to go down there to identify the body but I can't do it. I'm not going."

"Why?"

"Why! 'Cause once I identify the body I'll have to accept that Diamond is gone and she ain't coming back."

"I know what you mean. I'm not ready to accept it either but we don't have a choice." Before I could stop myself I broke down in tears. "I'm so sorry. I was trying to hold it together but I had so much love for your daughter and knowing I'll never see or talk to her again breaks my heart."

"Sweet Child, you don't have to apologize for loving my daughter."

"But you're her mother and my pain could never match yours. I should be trying to make you feel better instead you have to console me."

"Kennedy, stop being so hard on yourself, we'll both get through this," Ms. O'Toole reassured me, giving me a hug.

"I hope you're right."

"Of course I am. Would you like to go with me to identify the body?"

"I thought you said you weren't going."

"That's what my heart is telling me but in my mind I know better. I felt so connected to Diamond I always thought if anything like this ever happened to her I would be able to feel in my heart that she was gone. I think that's what makes this so hard to deal with, because deep down inside I don't feel like my baby has left me. But I know I have to accept that she has. Would you like to go with me so you can see her again and tell her goodbye?"

"Really? You wouldn't mind?"

"I wouldn't mind at all, actually I would appreciate

the support. I don't think I can do it alone."

"Ms. O'Toole, I would be honored to go with you. I came over here because I needed someone to share my pain with and who better than the person who loved her most in life. I thank you for helping me get through my pain." I held on tightly to Ms. O'Toole as we gave each other a warm hug. Diamond was gone but she would never be forgotten.

Blair

"I can't believe Diamond is gone," I wailed, as I lay on the floor in the fetal position.

"Blair, calm down," Skee kept repeating over and over again. After Kennedy confirmed my worst nightmare I fell to the floor and I couldn't stop crying.

"I can't calm down. My best friend is gone. She's gone forever. Why her...Diamond was all I had. She believed in me when no one else did. She did more for me than my own blood and now she's gone. This can't be my life."

Skee was kneeling down next to me with a combination of shock, confusion and remorse on his face. I could tell he wanted to make me feel better but he couldn't think of any words to say that would make that possible so instead he stood up and left me bawling like a baby. I wanted to stop hurting too but I couldn't, the stinging ran too deep. My tears continued to flow until my face started hurting as bad as my heart.

"Blair, I want to help you feel better," I heard Skee say as he came back into the bedroom.

"There's nothing you can do."

"I think I can help you." I shook my head no, knowing there was nothing he could do.

"There is nothing you can say to make this right. Please let me cry until I can't cry anymore."

"Baby, I hate to see you like this. But if you take two of these I promise it will take the pain away." Skee was now back kneeling down next to me holding two pills and a glass of water.

"Aspirin isn't going to make me better." Skee let out a slight chuckle.

"These are a lot stronger than aspirin and they're going to make you feel a lot better. Trust me...now take them." With the sort of misery I was in, I was willing to try just about anything to make it all stop. Between sobs I swallowed both pills hoping and praying the effects would kick in soon.

"Come on, lets get you off this floor," Skee said, lifting me up and laying me down in his bed. I balled up under the warm quilt and cried in the pillow. Skee sat at the edge of the bed and just watched me. I wasn't sure if he was waiting to see how long it would take for the pills to kick in or if he was worried about me or maybe it was a combination of both.

"You don't have to stay in here watching me," I mumbled through tears.

"If you don't mind I want to be near you. I feel for you right now. I really do. During my senior year in high school my best friend, the nigga I grew up with was murdered and I still haven't gotten over it. So trust me I know exactly how you're feeling. But it does get better."

"Really?"

"Yep. The initial pain is always the worse but in time it's not as bad. You'll never get completely over it but you will be able to move on with your life and find moments of happiness again."

"I pray you're right because this right here isn't for me. I don't like feeling this way."

"Well in about five more minutes you'll be feeling a lot better. That's why I gave you those pills. They really do come in handy in situations like this."

"Will you do me a favor?"

"Sure, what is it?"

"Will you come hold me?"

"Of course I will."

When Skee lay next to me and wrapped his arms around me, his warmth was exactly what I needed. After hearing about Diamond's death, I had never felt more alone in my life but having Skee hold me gave me comfort. Even if it was giving me a false sense of security, it was giving me exactly what I craved to ease me through my pain.

"You were right," I smiled. "Those five minutes must be here because I truly feel like I'm floating on a magical cloud."

"That's because you are," Skee said, smiling back.

"What kind of pills did I take?"

"Only the best...Opana. The euphoric properties in Opana is the most powerful you'll find in any pill on the market."

"Wow, is it legal?"

"Are you really that naive or are you playing with me?"

"Huh?" Skee gave me this peculiar half smile look.

I began laughing and I didn't know if it was from the affect of the pills or if I was just in a good mood. "I don't understand your question," I said, continuing to laugh.

"Lets just say that all pills are legal if prescribed by a physician and leave it at that."

"Got you. Do you think a doctor would give me a prescription for them? I mean this feels almost better than that Molly you gave me last night. Maybe better isn't the right word but different in a more relaxed, mellow way."

"Molly's are great for partying but you were depressed and hurting over the loss of your friend and I knew this would take the pain away."

"You were right. This is exactly what I needed," I said, leaning over to kiss Skee.

"Hold up." Skee put his hand on my shoulder and pushed me back with ease.

"Why did you push me away? I thought you liked kissing me."

"I do but I don't want a kiss like this. You're hurt about your friend and the pills got you feeling nice."

"If you're saying I don't know what I'm doing, you're wrong."

"I know you think you know what you're doing, but trust me it's important for us to wait. If you feel the same way when you're in a better place mentally, we'll try then. For now lie down and just let me hold you like you asked me to. Okay."

"Whatever you say." I cozied up against Skee's warm chiseled chest and before long I found myself dozing off to sleep. And for a moment all seemed perfect in the world.

Diamond

"Here, I brought you a change of clothes," Renny said, when he came in my room and sat a bag down on the edge of the bed.

"Thanks, does that mean I get to leave today and go home to my family?"

"That I'm not sure about."

"So what you haven't eliminated Tech and Parish yet?"

"Tech has been handled but Parish..." Renny gave an extended pause.

"What about Parish?"

"It's taking a little longer than I anticipated."

"What's the holdup?"

"Calm down. No worries, it will be handled."

"Renny, I want to go home to my family. I want to see my daughter, my mother and Cameron." Then I thought about if Blair and Kennedy heard the news. I knew Kennedy was strong but Blair she had always been somewhat fragile. Ever since we were kids I had to protect her. If she thought I wasn't going to be around anymore to be that rock she needed, I didn't know how she would take it.

"I understand, and you will but shit is real out here. These niggas ain't playin'. I have to make sure everything is straight before I send you back home."

"You know I appreciate you looking out for me but what's the hold up?"

"Honestly, Parish has been with Rico nonstop and my men haven't been able to take him down without having to take Rico out too. I know you don't fuck wit' dude like that but I also know you wouldn't want your daughter's father murdered either."

"You know me well," I said, putting my head down. "I can't stand Rico, but Destiny does love her dad and I wouldn't want his blood on my hands. Unless I find out that nigga was in on Parish robbing me."

"From everything we gathered it doesn't seem to be the case but I got my men checking, because if Rico was in on it the streets will be talking."

"When I confronted him about Parish he seemed genuinely stunned that I believed that he robbed me. But then again, I know first hand what a master liar Rico is."

"I tell you what. I'ma keep Parish as the sole target for now. Get rid of him so we can get you home and have these drug charges dropped against you. But I'll keep my ears open about Rico. If we find out he had anything to do with that robbery the nigga will be handled."

"That works for me."

"I figured it would. Listen, I'm sending one of the security men out to get you some food. Is there anything in particular you want?"

"Just some good breakfast food. I don't care what kind as long as it's yummy."

"I know the perfect spot."

"Great! I'ma take a shower and put on these clothes. Hopefully by then my food will be here."

"I'm sure it will. I have to step out too but I won't be gone long. I have a security man posted right outside your door though."

"Cool, I'll see you when you get back. Keeping my fingers crossed that you'll have good news for me when you return...you know that Parish has been deleted for good."

Renny simply nodded his head and left out my room. Without giving it a second thought I looked around for my purse, so I could get my wallet and look at a picture I kept of Destiny. I missed her so much and I just wanted to see her smile even if it wasn't the real deal. I thought it would help hold me over until I could have her in my arms again. Then just like that, the hope was ripped away from me when I remembered I didn't have my purse. It was left in my car with a dead body. I guess not remembering shit was a side affect from being stuck in a room all day and night.

All I could wish for was that Renny's men got rid of Parish sooner rather than later, because being shut off from the world was driving me crazy. I didn't even have a fuckin' television in my room. I wondered if Renny did that on purpose because he didn't want me to be able to watch the news. I somewhat understood, because listening to the media report dumb shit about me would've accomplished nothing, but piss me off further. I had no desire to keep feeling sorry for myself, so I grabbed the bag Renny left for me and headed to the bathroom to take a shower.

After taking my shower and getting dressed I was in the mirror, brushing my hair back into a ponytail when I heard banging on the bathroom door.

"Diamond, open the door! I heard a voice roar. I hesitated for a second until he said, "I'm Renny's security. He told me to come get you 'cause we have to go. Somehow they found out the location of the stash house and they coming for you!"

"Coming," I yelled out, quickly grabbing my things and tossing them in the bag.

"Yeah, Bitch, they coming for you a'ight." Those words and a Crimson Trace Laser Sight LG-417 Lasergrips Glock greeted me when I opened the door. I immediately recognized the model of the gun because I had one myself. It was too bad I didn't have it on me at this very moment because I desperately needed it.

"Parish, what are you doing here?"

"To kill yo' dumbass what the hell you think! Now come the fuck on," he belted, grabbing me by the ponytail I just spent a good deal of time getting done right.

"Yo, can you not pull on me so hard!" I screamed out.

"Shut the fuck up! You shoulda left well enough alone. You know gettin' robbed is part of the game in yo' line of business. If you would've took that L and kept it movin' I wouldn't be draggin' yo' ass right now. But naw, you had to see me dead. Now it's gon' be you they burying."

As Parish dragged me out I noticed a security guard that was posted right outside of my room, slumped over in a chair with a bullet to his head. Right then the tears started streaming down my face. I had escaped death once but this time it seemed I wouldn't be as lucky.

"If you' gon' kill me, do that shit right now," I barked, as if I was ready to die. God knew I wanted to live but at the same time I was trying to have some sort of control over my fate.

"All I have to do is pull the trigger and I can have yo' brains splattered across this wall but you wanna talk shit. I don't know if you bold or dumb. But no worries you will die today, but I'ma have a little fun wit' you before I take you out."

"What kinda fun?" I questioned Parish as he hauled me down the stairs.

"You'll see," he laughed. "Rico always talkin' 'bout you got that good pussy so I wanna see for myself," he continued in a taunting voice.

My stomach cramped up and I felt like I was about to vomit after he said that shit. In that instant I was about to say fuck it and start wilding out so the nigga could kill me right now on the spot. The thought of being violated by his punk ass seemed worse to me then having a bullet put through my head. But then I was struck by a glimmer of unexpected optimism. When we reached the bottom stair and Parish was pulling me around to go what I assumed to be a back exit, I noticed

Renny hiding in a corner holding a gun. He lifted his finger towards his mouth to motion me to stay quiet.

Parish was so busy laughing at his own sick jokes about all the foul shit he planned to do to me he wasn't even paying attention to his surroundings. He was being overly confident and I prayed it would be his downfall.

"How did you find me?" I decided to ask. I wanted his mind on other shit thinking it would keep him distracted so Renny could step in and kill the nigga with ease.

"You gon' die anyway so I guess it don't matter if I clue you in. One of the security men that works for yo' man Renny is my people. He hit me up last night and let me know you were here. He told me to wait and he would let me know the best time to snatch you up."

"So one of Renny's men clued you in?"

"What you hard of hearing...ain' that what I said."

"I'm just surprised one of Renny's men would turn on him like that."

"Don't nobody give a fuck 'bout Renny. That nigga think he run shit but he don't run nothin' 'round my way. My people, we look out for each other."

Parish continued to brag about how he was able to infiltrate Renny's stash house because of one of his disloyal men. It was obvious he was proud of his so-called accomplishment as he gloated over what went down. The next thing I knew he was opening the door for us to make our exit. The nervousness that had somewhat shifted away when I noticed Renny, was now back. I figured that because of the awkward way Parish had my body positioned it was difficult for Renny to get a clear shot. My mind was spinning and I needed to figure a way out of this because no matter what, I didn't want to get in the car with Parish.

"Can I please go to the bathroom before we leave?" I knew I was reaching but I was trying to stall for time and couldn't think of nothing else to say.

"Hell no! My people told me I had a short period of time to get yo' ass outta here. Somebody might show up any minute and I ain't takin' no chances, so move it!" he barked, pushing me forward. Parish was so busy trying to be extra with his manhandling that he lost his balance for a second when we were exiting out the back door.

I felt I had came to one of those now or never moments. I couldn't lie to myself I was scared shitless. If I made a break for it, even if Renny managed to get a good shot, Parish might be able to bust one off on me beforehand. But at this rate, Renny might completely miss an opportunity to take out Parish and there would be an even greater chance that I would end up dead. I decided to gamble with this moment and make my move. When Parish was trying to regain his balance, the hand that was holding the Glock came down near my face. With swiftness I lunged my mouth forward and pressed my teeth as deeply as I possibly could into the flesh of his hand. My grasp was so tight I know it had to feel like a Pit Bull was about to rip off his meat.

"You Biiiiiiiiiiiitch," Parish bawled, with agonizing pain, which caused him to drop his weapon. But that didn't cause the motherfucker to give up. The hand that had my ponytail wrapped around his fist, Parish freed and began punching me in my head like I was a straight up nigga in the street he was going toe-to-toe with. It then came down to the battle of the wills of who wanted to win this uneven fight the most. But I held in there, continuing to keep my teeth clenched like I was biting down into the last burger, and Parish wasn't letting up on his determination either as he kept blow after blow landing on my head. If I didn't die from a bullet I damn sure thought a concussion would take me out. Right when I felt I had reached my breaking point, I closed my eyes as everything went dark, then I heard a gunshot.

Kennedy

I held Ms. O'Toole's hand as we walked towards the office of the Chief Medical Examiner. My stomach was bubbling as I tried to mentally prepare myself to go identify Diamond's body.

"Did you ever hear back from Blair? Is she going to meet us here?" Ms. O'Toole asked, as we got closer to the building.

"She said she was. I sent her a text with the address so hopefully she'll get here in time."

"That would be good. I know how close she was to Diamond. They were like sisters," Ms. O'Toole said, tearing up.

I knew Ms. O'Toole wanted people who loved Diamond around her right now to give her strength, so I hoped Blair would make it in time. Right then I noticed a chauffeured driven Bentley pulling up. I couldn't see who was in the back because of the dark tinted window. After a few minutes Blair stepped out.

"I'm so glad you made it," Ms. O'Toole smiled when Blair walked up, giving her a hug.

"Of course. When Kennedy told me you all would

be here I had to come."

"It's good that you're here," I said, kissing Blair on the cheek. "Did you come by yourself?" I questioned, curious to know whose car she came in.

"No, Skee came with me but he thought he should wait in the car and give us time alone." What Blair said caught me by surprise. I had a ton of questions to ask her but decided this wasn't the right time and thought it best to wait until after we weren't around Ms. O'Toole.

Once we got inside the surprises kept coming when I spotted Cameron speaking to a woman. "Isn't that Cameron," Blair commented, noticing him too.

"Yeah, it is. I had no idea he would be here, did you, Ms. O'Toole?"

"No I didn't."

Cameron must've felt our presence because after a few seconds he turned in our direction. He then turned back towards the woman he was speaking to, said a few more words and came walking towards us. As he got closer he looked really bad as if he hadn't had any sleep and his eyes were bloodshot.

"Hey, we were surprised to see you here."

"My lawyer called me this morning and told me that Diamond's body hadn't been identified and that you said you weren't going to be able to do it," Cameron said, looking at Ms. O'Toole. "Ms. O'Toole, I understood why. So I thought it would be easier on everybody if I just came and did it."

"That was very sweet of you, Cameron. Initially I did tell the police I couldn't come, but after talking to Kennedy I changed my mind. Have you already done it?"

she asked in a low tone as if not ready to say Diamond's name.

"No not yet. I was about to when you all walked in."

"If you all don't mind I want to go in first. I would like a moment alone with my daughter."

"We understand. We'll be here waiting for you." We all stood there with our heads down for what seemed like forever and the mood was beyond bleak. I finally decided to say something because the complete silence was about to drive me insane.

"I think it's really good that the three people who were closes to Diamond, besides her mother and daughter of course are all here together."

"Yes, I think so too. Diamond would want us to support each other during a time like this," Cameron added. "But honestly I still can't believe she is really gone. I keep on thinking this is some sorta fucked up joke. I mean who would want to kill Diamond. She was the sweetest girl I knew. Never hurt anybody."

"I know and she was always there for everybody. If you needed anything and she could help you she would. Diamond helped everybody and there was nobody there to help..." Before I could complete my sentence Blair burst out in tears. "Blair, it's okay," I said rubbing her shoulder.

"No it's not," she said, as the tears continue to pour. "You're right. Diamond always helped everybody else and I should've done something to help her too."

"What are you talking about?" Cameron asked, stepping closer to Blair. "Do you know something about what happened to her?"

"We were best friends and when she confided in me I...." Blair's voice started to crack in mid sentence.

"You what?" Cameron's voice was rising. "What did she confide in you and say?"

"Yeah, Blair what did Diamond tell you? If you know something about who might've killed her you need to tell us," I pleaded.

"Diamond told me..." Before Cameron and I could hear what Blair had to say we heard a woman screaming.

"That isn't my baby, that isn't my baby!" We all glanced up and saw Ms. O'Toole running down the hall. We ran towards her to find out what she was talking about.

"Ms. O'Toole calm down," Cameron said in a gentle voice taking her hand.

"That's not Diamond in there. That's not my baby girl's body in there."

"Huh, what are you talking about?" I was baffled by what she was saying.

"You heard me. That body I went to identify is not Diamond's. I don't know who that is, but she's not my daughter. My baby is alive! I know it!"

Blair

"I can't believe that Diamond may actually still be alive."

"Me neither but it damn sure looks that way. One thing we do know for sure, that dead body we saw was not Diamond."

"But how did she end up in Diamond's car with her purse. This is all so bizarre," I said, shaking my head before taking a sip of the champagne I was cradling in my hand.

"Exactly and if Diamond is alive why hasn't she gotten in touch with any of us. That might not have been Diamond's body, but something is definitely wrong."

"For sure but what?"

"Maybe what you were about to tell Cameron and I yesterday could help us figure it out."

"What I was about to tell you guys…I don't know what you're talking about."

"You know, about Diamond confiding in you."

"Oh, that." I tried to act nonchalant. I was hoping that with all the drama that went on yesterday at the Medical Examiner's office, Kennedy would've forgotten about my breakdown. Now that there was a chance

Diamond was alive I had no intentions of revealing what she had told me. I had a moment of weakness because of guilt but now that my mind was clear I would take her secret to the grave with me.

"Yeah that, so what did Diamond tell you that had you all choked up?"

"She had confided in me that when she got arrested it was bothering her a lot more than she was letting on because she didn't want to concern you and Cameron. I felt maybe I should've told her to be honest with you guys instead of keeping it to herself. And when you brought up that she was always helping others it just brought all these emotions. You know, because Diamond was always being so strong for everybody."

"Yeah she was. I'm just praying that wherever she is, she's safe."

"Me too because I don't think I can take losing her all over again. As you can see I've completely lost my appetite behind this shit," I said, looking down at the food I ordered but hadn't touched."

"So Skee Patron is getting you through this difficult time?"

"I like how smoothly you slid that question in there."

"Listen, I was stunned when you told me he was in the car waiting for you, but yesterday we didn't have time to discuss it. So after the party you spent the night with him?"

"Well let's jump right in with the questions! Yeah, after you called me about Diamond I think I kinda blacked out and Skee took me back to his place. He's been really sweet."

"So you're falling for him?"

"Maybe, I don't know. He's easy to be around which is what I need after dealing with Michael for all this time."

"Speaking of Michael, he called giving me the 3rd degree about you being on the red carpet with Skee. That man has serious control issues."

"Yes, he left a bunch of messages on my phone about that. I don't have the energy to deal with Michael right now. Until I find out what happened to Diamond I don't know how much I'll be able to deal with."

"I figured that so I rescheduled your audition in LA."

"Fuck I totally forgot about that!"

"Marcus was very understanding."

"Yeah, 'cause those Hollywood types normally don't give a fuck. What's that saying...the show must go on. But you know work might be exactly what I need to get me through this."

"Well he didn't give us a lot of time, only a couple of weeks. But that's better than nothing and he only gave me that because he really does think you'll be perfect for this role."

"I pray we find Diamond before then but even if we don't I'll be ready. I know Diamond would want me to go to Hollywood and kick ass."

"No doubt. But I think we're going to find out something soon."

"What makes you so sure?"

"Now that we know that wasn't Diamond,

Cameron has hired the best private detective to find out what happened to her. He'll probably get to the bottom of it before the NYPD."

"I feel so bad for him. He's taking this really hard."

"The two of them are so in love. If anybody can find her it will be Cameron."

"True. So you ready to go, because I'm tired of looking at this cold food and I refuse to drink one more glass of champagne on an empty stomach."

"Yes. But I have to make a stop. I'll see you later on at the apartment."

"I'll probably be gone by the time you get there."

"You have a date tonight?"

"I wouldn't call it a date but I'ma spend the night at Skee's place."

"Excuse me?"

"What's up with the frown? You're the one who set me up with him."

"Yeah for publicity, not for you to fall in love."

"I didn't say I was in love with him."

"That's what your mouth is saying, but your eyes are saying something else."

"Would it be so bad if I fell in love with Skee Patron? I mean he is a superstar."

"Sometimes I forget how naive you are."

"And what does that mean?"

"What it means is that the ride Michael took you on will seem like child's play compared to the rollercoaster you'll be on fuckin' around with Skee Patron."

"You're crazy. Skee is nothing like Michael."

"Yeah you're right, Skee's worse but in a different

way. He's worshipped by millions of fans. His level of narcissism has no limits. Trust me I know. When I worked for Darcy all I dealt with were stars and most of them weren't half as successful as Skee, but thought the world revolved around them. But you really are dealing with a superstar that the world does revolve around... are you following me?"

"I hear you but you're wrong about Skee."

"Just be careful, Blair. You went through so much with Michael. I would hate for you to get out of one bad situation and jump right into a nightmare."

"I appreciate your concern but trust me Skee only wants what is best for me. He wants me to be happy."

"For your sake I hope you're right."

"Ahhhh, don't stop," I moaned as Skee's tongue danced on my clit while Aaliyah's *I Don't Wanna* played in the background. This was our third time having sex in the last few hours and it still felt just as good as the first time. As if reading my mind his tongue exited between my legs and he slid his massive dick inside of me in its place.

"How that feel?" he asked, already knowing the answer.

"Perfect. I wish you could stay inside of me forever," I admitted, wrapping my legs even tighter around him kissing his neck. Each stroke was getting more and more intense. "Oh, baby, keep going just like that. I think I'm about to cum."

"Can I choke you?"

"What did you say?" I thought I heard what he said, but I wanted to be sure because I was taken aback.

Skee stared at me directly in my eyes and said, "Can I choke you while you're about to cum?" For some crazy reason his request turned me on even more than I already was.

"Yes."

"You sure." I reached up putting my tongue down his throat wanting to kiss him. Our kiss became even more passionate until he suddenly stopped. "Answer me. Are you sure?"

"Yes, I'm sure. Do it...choke me. I'm about to cum." I lay there and willingly let Skee wrap his hands around my neck and choke me as a powerful tingling sensation shot though my entire body. The pressure of him strangling me seemed to heighten my pleasure. After we reached our climax we fell asleep with Skee still lying inside of me.

Diamond

After I heard the gunshot go off, it took me a second to open my eyes and realize the bullet didn't hit me. I think because I was still in pain from the pounding my head took, it was taking a moment for me to process everything. When my eyes did focus on my surroundings I saw Parish face down on the ground moaning in agony. Renny quickly ran up on Parish with his gun pointed directly at him. He took his foot and turned him over on his back.

Even with death lingering over his head Parish wanted to pop shit. "Fuck both of you motherfuckers," he mumbled with blood running out his mouth.

I grabbed the Glock that Parish had dropped when I bit down on his hand and aimed it at his head. I was ready to make sure his ass was dead once and for all. "Nigga, you picked the wrong Bitch to rob," I spit, ready to take him out.

"Go right ahead and kill me but I'ma die wit' a smile on my face knowing yo' own baby daddy set you up to be robbed. He even gave me permission to smash the pussy," Parish said, before letting out a menacing chuckle. Before he could utter another word I pulled the trigger, making sure it was lights out forever for that bum ass nigga.

"Rico's ass is next," I stated, as venom occupied every inch of my body.

"I'll take care of it."

"No, Renny, that is one murder I want to take complete credit for. I will be the last face Rico sees before he dies."

I stood outside the door for a few minutes before using my key to open it. I had already seen my mother and Destiny. I already spoke to Blair and Diamond. The only person left was Cameron and this reunion made me the most nervous. I had practiced what I planned to say over and over again that the story should roll off my tongue but I knew when I looked Cameron in his eyes that there was a chance it could all go wrong. But standing in the hallway wasn't going to make it any easier so I took a deep breath and went inside.

"You really are alive." Those were the first words out of Cameron's mouth when I walked through the door.

"Yes I am." We slowly walked towards each other as if this was the first time we had ever laid eyes on one another and wanted to study each physical attribute we had. Then we met right in the center of the room and Cameron lifted me up, holding me so close that I thought our bodies had become one.

"Don't ever do this to me again. I don't think I

could live without you."

"I won't. I promise. Before any other words were exchanged our kisses spoke for us. Those kisses led us to our bed and making love like this could be our last time, so we wanted it to be our best. It didn't even feel real but instead magical. Our lovemaking had been so intense that we fell asleep in each other's arms without even speaking about what happened, that was until we woke up the next morning.

"Diamond, where were you when you went missing for those couple days and why didn't you call me?" My back was up against Cameron when he asked the question so he couldn't see the expression on my face. His strong arms were holding me close and my eyes darted around the room as I thought carefully before I answered. I wanted to make sure I chose my words correctly and stuck to the script I had already written in my head.

"I couldn't call you."

"Why?"

"I left my cell in my truck and where I was I didn't have access to a phone."

"Where were you?"

"I was at a safe house?"

"Who had you there?"

"The police."

"What? But they thought you were dead."

"That's what they wanted everybody to believe until they could figure out who was trying to kill me."

"So they were in on it the entire time and put us through hell making us think you were dead. What sick fucks!" Cameron rose up as his anger started to get the best of him.

"Cameron, let me finish explaining." I knew I had to deescalate his fury before he flipped out, went investigating and found out more than I wanted him to know.

"What is there to explain? The cops knew you weren't dead but purposely let us think you were."

"In the very beginning they did think I was dead. This girl named Tisha who I was cool with lied to me so I would meet up with her. The dead body in my car was her and because my purse and other belongings were left there too, they assumed she was me. But I was left in the trunk unconscious, and by the time they found me some unknown source had already leaked to the press that I was the dead woman in the car."

"I'm lost."

"I know when I woke up and the officer assigned to watch over me while I was at the safe house explained what happened I was confused too. They said they believe the woman who knocked me out put my body in the trunk and was planning to take me, who knows where but whoever shot up my truck killed her before she could do so. They probably thought she was me. Putting me in that trunk saved my life."

"So somebody was trying to kill you but killed some other woman instead?"

"Exactly."

"So that means your life is still in danger?"

"No. That's why the police kept me at the safe house and didn't want the person responsible to know

I was still alive until they had everything under control. They didn't want to take any chances. But I'm good now so they let me come home."

"So who was behind this bullshit?"

"You were right from the very beginning. It was Destiny's dad. He was behind all of it."

"I knew it was yo' sorry ass baby daddy. He set you up on those bogus drug charges too didn't he?"

"Yep, he sure did."

"That motherfucker better be glad his punk ass locked up or I swear I would have him killed."

"The police haven't arrested him yet, but trust he will get his."

"What the fuck are they waiting on?"

"They're just making sure their case is solid so he won't be able to beat the charges. But they have multiple officers watching him every minute of the day so I'm safe. If I weren't they wouldn't of let me come home. But, baby I've told you way more than I was supposed to. One of the conditions of them letting me come home was that I promised not to reveal any of this. They want to make sure their case against Rico isn't compromised."

"As much as I want that nigga handled I won't say shit. I'll let the police do their job but if they come up short he will be dealt with."

"Thank you. I knew I could trust you."

"Always. Diamond, you can tell me anything. I'll always have your back. You're my baby and I love you."

"Cameron, you have no idea how much that means to me. I love you too."

Kennedy

"Kennedy, you always pick the best restaurants. I heard so much about this place but I've never been here."

"I can't take credit for this spot. It was Blair's idea. Speaking of Blair, where the hell is she?" I questioned, looking down at my watch.

"That's a good question. Blair's not the most punctual person but she's not normally this late."

"Yeah, and she can't say it's because she didn't know the address. She's the one that told me this place was 33 East 60th Street on Madison Avenue. Like she had the shit memorized."

"I'm sure she'll be here soon."

"I hope so because I'm sure the waiter is ready to take our order and I don't want to another drink until I get some food on my stomach."

"Speaking of the devil, here comes my bestie now," Diamond said, nodding her head towards the stairs.

"Hi, ladies! I apologize for my tardiness," Blair giggled. She gave both of us air kisses and sat down. I hadn't seen much of Blair in the last couple of weeks because she had been spending most of her time with

Skee but something seemed different about her. I couldn't put my finger on it though.

"We're glad you made it, we're starving."

"Me too. But I promise you're going to love it. Philippe's food is incredible."'

"How did you find out about this place?"

"Skee. We eat here almost every other night. We can't get enough. I think I'll have the duck. But that takes about 45 minutes for them to cook. I have an idea we'll get a little bit of everything and share it. How does that sound?"

"Works for me what about you, Kennedy?"

"I'm down."

"That was easy. Now all we have to do is wait for the waiter to come back," Diamond laughed.

"Exactly, but we have so much to talk about, we can keep ourselves busy until he comes back."

"This is the first time the three of us have all been out together since I returned from my little situation."

"That's cute how you described that...little situation," Blair giggled again, playfully slapping Diamond's arm.

"You're in an awfully jolly mood, Blair. I guess things must be going well between you and Skee. But I should've known that since you've practically moved in with him."

"Kennedy, you sure know how to exaggerate. I haven't moved in with Skee."

"We'll you certainly haven't been at my place, so I'm assuming you've been at his place."

"Yes I have but it's no big deal."

"Sounds like a big deal to me. I didn't realize you and Skee Patron were so serious."

"Diamond, don't you fall for how dramatic Kennedy is being. We just enjoy each other's company."

"I know you've been having so much fun, but don't forget we leave for LA in a couple days."

"Kennedy, of course I haven't forgotten."

"So you're prepared and ready for the audition?" I didn't even try to hide my skepticism.

"What type of question is that?"

"A good one. Now please answer it."

"Here comes our waiter. Let me order our food." I watched and listened to Blair go through the menu and order practically everything on there. For somebody that claimed to be eating here every other night, Blair didn't look like she had gained a pound. If anything she seemed to have lost a few. But a weight loss didn't seem to be what was different about her.

"So are you ready to answer my question?" I jumped right back to what we were discussing once Blair was finished ordering and the waiter left.

"Yes, Kennedy, I'm ready for the audition. My bags are already packed."

"Your bags are packed...where are they at Skee's place."

"As a matter of fact they are."

"Blair, you don't think you're moving a little fast with Skee? You got out of a relationship with Michael like yesterday and now you're shacking up with Skee."

"It just happened okay. Plus it's nice to sleep in a bed opposed to Kennedy's couch. No offense to your couch, Kennedy."

"None taken."

"All I'm saying is as much as I appreciate you letting me stay with you when I left Michael, being with Skee is nice. I don't know how long this arrangement is going to last but he doesn't want me to go and honestly I don't want to go either."

"As long as Skee knows that if you get this part in the movie, you'll be leaving whether he likes it or not."

"Duh, plus he's about to go back on tour anyway. He has his own life and he wants me to have mine. We're on the same page about everything. Now enough about Skee and me lets talk about something else. Diamond, how's Destiny, your mom and Cameron?"

"They're great! I didn't think it could get any better but things are super between Cameron and me. It's like my little situation brought us even closer together."

"I'm so happy for you"

"So am I, Diamond. He was torn up when we thought something bad happened to you. He really is in love with you."

"The feeling is mutual. I couldn't have asked for a more perfect man. Speaking of perfection, check out who just walked in." Blair and I both looked up and turned in the direction Diamond was staring. All three of us watched as Kirk walked past our table with some chick. He acknowledged Diamond with a nod, but I caught him giving Blair a glare dripping with disgust.

"Blair, what was that look about?"

"I peeped that too," Diamond chimed in. "Did something go down between you and Kirk that you never shared with us?"

"It happened the night of that party."

"What party?"

"That party Kennedy set me up on with Skee."

"What happened?"

"Kirk saw me there with Skee and we got a little carried away."

"Carried away?"

"Yeah, the champagne was flowing we were feeling good and we started making out. Kirk came over and felt some type of way about it."

"Let me get this straight, some champagne you were drinking, had you feeling so good that you started making out with Skee at the club in front of everybody."

"Yeah, something like that."

"How many bottles of champagne did you have... three."

"Don't be sarcastic, Kennedy."

"I'm not. I'm serious. I've been out with you many times and never have I seen you so open off of champagne that you would make out with a man in public, especially one that you barely knew at the time."

"I have to agree with Kennedy. That doesn't sound like you at all. Even during the times you were happy with Michael I never saw you show public affection. You've always been on the reserved side."

"It's not that I'm reserved, Skee just brings out the affectionate side of me."

"I must find out these magical powers Skee seems to have over you."

"Or maybe the magic is what's in his pants,"

Diamond teased.

"There is definitely some magic down there," Blair laughed. "But here comes our food. Kennedy, can you please put a halt on your Skee interrogation until after we finish eating."

"No interrogation here. Only trying to wrap my mind around how Skee is able to make you feel completely uninhibited."

"I think it's great Skee is able to bring her out of her shell. I've been trying to do it forever with no luck. So kudos to Skee."

"Thank you, Diamond. Let's toast to that. Come on, Kennedy, raise your glass too." I reluctantly obliged. "To Skee, for bringing me out of my shell and giving me the courage to live my life and have fun! Now lets eat!"

I decided to put an end to my fishing expedition and played along with the cheerful toast Blair gave. Blair and I were headed to LA in a couple days and she was about to audition for the biggest role of her life so far and I wanted her to stay in a great mood. If Skee was responsible for making that happen then so be it. I would much rather her be upbeat than always half depressed and insecure like she was when she was with Michael.

"Girl, you were right, this food is freakin' ridiculously good."

"I told you."

"Yeah you did but you've barely touched your food."

"I ate some of my food, but this champagne killed my hunger."

"Well whatever, more food for us."

"True, oh gosh I have to go anyway. Skee is outside."

"I thought this was supposed to be a girl's night out?"

"It has been. We've chatted had dinner but I promised Skee I would go to this party with him tonight. You know I'm about to go to LA. He wants to get some time in before I leave."

"I understand. Give me a hug and kiss before you go. I'll call you tomorrow."

"Thanks, Diamond. You guys enjoy the rest of your night and I'll see you in a couple days, Kennedy, so we can catch that flight."

"Cool, but I'll be talking to you before then."

"Of course you will. Bye ladies!" Blair waved before walking down the stairs to make her exit.

"I've never seen her so happy. Skee might be exactly what Blair needed."

"Or maybe not."

"What's up with the negativity? Why don't you like Skee?"

"I don't dislike him but I'm not sure if he's a good fit for Blair."

"It's not like they're about to walk down the aisle. She's having fun and after that horrific Michael I'm thrilled she met a man that can put a smile on her face."

"You're right."

"Of course I am. I'm always right," Diamond boasted, before we both laughed and continued to enjoy our meal.

Blair

"That's the dress I want you to wear," Skee stated, as I stood in front of the mirror. This was the fifth dress I tried on and at this point I was relieved he finally picked one he liked.

"I like this one too. You picked all these out yourself or did you have a stylist do it?"

"Of course I picked them out myself. There's no stylist that's gonna know what I like better than me. Plus, I know what I want to see my woman in."

"So I'm your woman now," I giggled, as he walked by me kissing my lips.

"In that dress you better be." There was no denying the skintight white Kaufmanfranco gown was stunning. The long slit that went all the way up the back is what sealed the deal for me. "Are you ready?"

"Yes I am. Let me grab my purse and we can go."

"What time does your flight leave tomorrow?"

"Noon. I told Kennedy I would meet her at the airport so I should probably leave here about ten, to be on the safe side."

"I already put my driver on alert so we're good."

"You said we're, so you're riding to the airport with me?"

"I planned to is that a problem?"

"Of course not. I just didn't think you would feel like it. Are you going to miss me, is that what it is?" I teased, stroking the side of Skee's face.

"As a matter of fact I am. If you weren't coming right back I would go with you."

I paused for a moment and took in what Skee said. It wasn't his answer that threw me off so much, but the genuineness on his face. Was it possible that this thing we had going meant more to him than just a fun fling? I knew we enjoyed each other's company but I figured I was just the it girl of the moment and that was cool with me. After Michael I wanted to be with somebody I could let my hair down with and have fun. Skee gave me exactly that and more. But maybe I was reading way too much into this.

"I'm gonna miss you too. But I'm coming right back so don't try to replace me," I smiled.

"Never you're irreplaceable. Now lets go. If I have to look at you standing there in that dress any longer it's coming off."

"That doesn't sound like such a bad idea."

"Trust me, later tonight that's exactly what's going down," Skee said, wrapping his arm around my waist as we headed out the bedroom.

When we pulled in front of the townhouse on East 78th Street, I thought maybe we were picking somebody up until the driver came around to open my door. "Babe, I thought we were going to a party?"

"We are, it's here."

"At this townhouse?"

"Yeah, it's a private Hush party. They give them twice a year. You don't know the location until a couple hours prior. These are some of the most exclusive parties of the year. That's why I wanted to make sure you were the best thing in there tonight and with that dress you will be."

Skee pulled out his cell phone showing the security officer a text message before we were allowed to enter. "I can't believe you have to show somebody a text message to get into a party."

"I told you it was exclusive. They're very strict which I like. That means we can feel comfortable to do whatever the hell we wanna do because they made sure not to let any outsiders in."

"Wow this place is humongous," I said looking around at what had to be at least 13,000 square feet of living space. We were escorted to what must've been an additional entertaining terrace on the very top floor of the eight levels home. Luckily there was elevator access to all floors or somebody could easily pass out trying to maneuver around.

We walked through what seemed to be a small tunnel and when we reached a tall-carved stone door. When the door was opened it was like we left New York City and entered the nightlife of Miami. There were cabanas surrounding a shimmering pool, with lavish gold-plated designs that were clearly inspired by the female body.

"Is that a champagne waterfall?" There were a group of people surrounding a waterfall and they kept filling their glasses up.

"Yeah it is. It's nice right..."

"I would describe it a little better than nice." I had never seen anything like this place in my life. It was beyond extravagant and if I wasn't seeing all this for myself, I wouldn't believe it existed.

"Come this way," Skee said taking my hand. "I see our table over there." As we made our way through the crowd Skee was speaking to several people he knew and I recognized some too. There was a mixture of A List people you would see at the Oscars, the Grammy's, the ESPN sports awards and then throw in some politicians. It was truly a party of the who's who.

Once we were seated at our table, a scantly clad waitress immediately approached to take our drink order. "Would you like to try our specialty cocktail called "The One"?"

"What's in it?"

"It's a mix of a rare Dom Perignon champagne and a shot of Louis XII Remy Martin Black Pearl cognac."

"Yes, bring us a few of those," Skee jumped in, answering for me. "Are you enjoying yourself yet?"

"I'm still in a state of shock. I've been to some pretty great parties, but none of them come remotely close to this."

"Just stay by my side. We'll travel the world together and you can see it all. Now it's time for us to have some fun."

"Yes, lets have some fun," I beamed, taking the Molly, Skee handed me.

"I'll be right back...you good?"

"Yeah I'm good." And I was until less than thirty seconds after Skee walked off, I noticed Kirk walking directly towards me. I tried to pretend I didn't even notice him so he would hopefully make a beeline right past me, but no such luck.

"So I guess you and Skee are a couple now."

"Is that the new greeting? What happened to how are you or how are you doing?"

"I just want to know."

"Know what?"

"All that time when I thought we were trying to build something, were you actually seeing Skee?"

"No. When I met you I was still seeing Michael. There was nothing between Skee and me. It just happened. And honestly I hate what has happened between us. I thought at the very least we would always have a friendship."

"I can't watch my friend's pop pills and not try to make them stop."

"What are you talking about?"

"Before I walked over here, I watched you take that pill from Skee and put it in your mouth. I bet that's what you were on that night I saw you at the party and you wasn't actin' like yo'self."

"Would you stop! You don't know anything about me."

"I know this pill poppin' party girl, runnin' 'round with Skee Patron isn't the girl I met and thought was special."

"Kirk, please don't do this. We're at a party and all I want to do is enjoy myself. Have some fun. Is that so wrong?"

"When this everyday all day long party you're on with Skee is over with, give me a call, because I miss my friend." Kirk gave me this look of disappointment before walking away.

"Can you bring some more drinks please," I told the waitress as I gulped down the two that were on the table. Kirk came over fucking up my high and I was desperately trying to get it back. When I thought my night couldn't get anymore fucked up, I looked up to see Michael staring down at me.

"Why the fuck haven't you been answering my calls. I've left you numerous messages."

"Clearly I have nothing to say to you."

"Who the fuck are you here with?"

"Michael, I don't report to you anymore. Remember I moved out."

"Yeah, so you could go sleep on the couch at that girl's rundown apartment."

"Whatever, Michael. The point is I'm not at your place. I'm not getting a dime from you so I owe you nothing."

"You're drunk that's why you're acting like this. So I'll excuse your behavior."

"Blair, is everything good over here?"

"I'm sure you know who I am. I'm Michael Frost."

"Actually I don't. But I'm here checkin' on my girl. Blair are you..."

"Your girl?" Michael questioned cutting Skee off.

"Yeah, that's what I said, *my girl*," he stressed. "You have a problem wit' that?"

"Is that true, Blair. You're a rapper's girl now."

"Nigga, what the fuck you just say."

"Stop, both of you and Michael please go," I practically begged, as I stood between them.

"I don't want to cause any problems at this party so I'll excuse myself. But so you know, my man," Michael added in his most arrogant condescending voice. "After Blair gets whatever you all have going on out of her system, she'll be back. She always comes back to me."

"I'ma fuck that nigga up!" Skee shouted lunging towards Michael. Luckily some men that were cool with Skee saw what was transpiring, stepped in and held him back.

"Babe, sit down. We can't let Michael fuck up our night."

"That's your ex you told me about, wasn't it?"

"Yes and he's my ex for a reason. So please we can't let him fuck up our high."

"You're right. Fuck him."

"Exactly! Now give me another Molly. We're supposed to be having the most fun ever before I leave tomorrow. Don't mess that up for me. For us."

"You're right, baby," Skee said before putting his tongue in my mouth and we embraced for a long passionate kiss. Before long we had forgotten all about Michael's bullshit and we were back poppin' Molly's, drinking champagne and dancing our asses off. It was definitely turning into a night to remember.

I could barely lift my head as I rubbed my eyes trying to wake up. I almost said forget it and lay back down so I could sleep for a few more hours but then something triggered in my brain that I had a flight to catch. I squinted my eyes around the room trying to see what time it was but I didn't see a clock and my surroundings seemed so unfamiliar. The only reason I didn't panic was because I did notice Skee lying next to me in the bed. I then reached around trying to locate my cell and I finally found it under my dress that was on the floor. My heart completed dropped when I saw all the missed calls and text messages from Kennedy and my phone said 4:29pm.

"Fuck...fuck...fuck!" Was all I could get out before falling back in the bed.

Diamond

"Diamond, have you spoken to Blair?"

"No. You still haven't been able to get in touch with her?"

"Hell no! I can't believe Blair never showed up to the airport and isn't answering her phone. What the fuck! You don't think something bad happened to her do you? I'm getting worried."

"Did you try calling Skee?"

"Of course I did! I even had his publicist call him and she didn't get an answer."

"I wasn't going to say anything, but since you still haven't been able to reach her."

"Say anything about what?"

"Cameron told me that he heard they were at a party last night together."

"What party? I checked everything that was going on in the city last night. Skee and Blair weren't at anything."

"This wasn't some standard industry event. It was something called a Hush party. Some real exclusive shit."

"Fuck! That's why neither one of them are

answering their phones. They are probably passed out drunk somewhere. This can't be my life. Out of all the nights for her to go out and get drunk, why last night when we had a flight to catch today."

"Kennedy, calm down. You said her audition isn't until the morning. You all can get on another flight."

"Some major corporate convention is going on in LA and mostly all the flights are booked. It was a miracle we were both able to get on the twelve o'clock flight. I can try to see what I can find but first I have to talk to her. It's after four and still no word."

"Has anybody gone over to his crib?"

"Yes, his publicist and she said nobody is home. I don't know if she's lying. All I do know is Blair is a no show and if we're not at that studio tomorrow morning for the audition, she can kiss that role goodbye."

"I have to head out but I'll keep trying to get in touch with Blair. As soon as I hear from her, I'll give you a call and vice versa."

When I hung up with Kennedy I felt terrible. She had busted her ass to get Blair's career to a point that she could get an audition like this and now it seemed to be slipping right through her fingers. Maybe Kennedy was right, that Skee wasn't a good influence for Blair. But I had never seen her so happy and it all seemed to be because of Skee.

"Is everything okay?" hearing Cameron's voice startled me out of my thoughts.

"No. Kennedy still hasn't been able to get in touch with Blair and she's worried they won't make it to LA in time for the audition."

"Wow, that's fucked up. Maybe this is Blair's way of saying she doesn't want to go and she's over this whole acting Hollywood shit."

"I don't think so. Blair has wanted this for so long and so bad. She's always dreamed of being a famous actress. I think she just got caught up with hanging out with Skee."

"Yeah that dude is on some larger than life shit."

"What you mean?"

"From what I hear, he really lives that rockstar life to the fullest, a nonstop party. I don't see how Blair can pursue a legitimate acting career and be his girl at the same time. One is gonna have to go. Maybe by not showing up, Blair chooses him."

"I hope you're wrong. But listen I have to run a few errands so I'll be back later on."

"Don't forget about our dinner date tonight."

"I did forget, what time?"

"Seven. And, baby, please don't be late. I have a surprise for you."

"What kind of surprise?"

"If I tell you it wouldn't be a surprise now would it."

"I'm excited! I thought we were doing the regular go out to eat thing but now you're saying it's a surprise dinner. Can you at least give me a hint?"

"Nope. All I'm going to say is wear something extra beautiful tonight," Cameron said, leaning down giving me a kiss before I left.

When I got to Queens, I sat in the rental car I got so I wouldn't be seen as I watched Rico's every move. For the last couple weeks I had been letting the chaos die down as I strategized the perfect time for me to make my move. If I had my way Rico would already be dead but I knew that patience was the key. I had planned to see if today could be the day but Cameron's reminder of our dinner date tonight shut that shit down. Killing Rico and getting back home in time for a night out with Cameron was playing it way too close. But observing him and plotting my next move would have to hold me over and it would. Knowing Rico would be a dead man soon enabled me to calm all my nerves.

Kennedy

"Where the fuck are you!" I yelled into the phone when Blair finally called.

"Kennedy, calm down."

"How the hell are you going to tell me to calm down when you're about to kill your career before it even has a chance to start."

"I understand you're upset and you have every right to be. I accidentally overslept and I apologize."

"Save that weak ass apology! I know you were out partying all night at that Hush party. You have your priorities all fucked up."

"Listen, I made a mistake and all I want to do now is make it right."

"I can't find any flights that will get us to LA in time for the audition. Right before you called I was about to call Marcus and let him know we weren't going to be able to make it."

"Kennedy, don't do that."

"Blair, don't you get it, it's over. You've fucked up royally and I can't fix this."

"You're right, I did fuck up but we are going to fix it."

"And how do you plan on doing that, because you calling Marcus and begging him to give you another chance after he already rescheduled once for you isn't going to work."

"We're not going to reschedule. Skee is going to let us use his private jet. We're leaving tonight."

"Excuse me!" I didn't even try to hide the excitement in my voice. "Did you just say that Skee was letting us take his private jet?"

"Yes. He's already arranged everything. All we have to do is stop by his place, get my luggage, then come pick you up and we're out."

"So where are you now?"

"We spent the night at the townhouse where the party was. But we're about to leave shortly. We should be to you in the next hour or so. I'll call you when we're on our way."

"Blair, please don't fuck this up."

"I'm not. You have every right to be pissed but I'm going to make this right. I promise...see you soon."

When I ended my call with Blair I quickly hit up Diamond. "Hallelujah we're back in the game!"

"You finally talked to Blair?"

"Yes! And Skee is going to let us use his private jet so we can get to LA in time for the audition."

"Wow! So I guess he isn't as bad as you thought."

"Right now at this stage in Blair's career I don't think Skee is the best fit for her but hey he really did come through. I mean I don't know anybody that can let me use their private plane, so I guess having a superstar boyfriend has its perks."

"It sure seems that way. So when are you guys leaving?"

"Blair said they'd be coming to pick me up in an hour or so."

"Does that mean Skee is coming with you guys?"

"You know I got that feeling, but I didn't want to ask and sound like I had a problem with him coming, especially since it's his plane."

"Would you be uncomfortable?"

"Why, if I am does that mean you'll come? I mean I'm sure nobody would have a problem adding one more person to the flight."

"I would love to make that trip with you all but Cameron has a surprise dinner for me tonight. I can't wait to spend some quality time with my man because he actually is heading out of town tomorrow. But you'll be fine."

"Honestly I'm not worried about me. I'm more concerned about Blair. I want her to focus on being ready for the audition. Skee strikes me as the type that he would want all her focus to be on him when he's around."

"Sounds about right, but you'll have to remind Blair what the bigger picture is. This is the type of role that can change her life."

"And that is what I plan to do. Now let me get off this phone. Now that I know we're back in business, let me get my shit together so I'll be ready when they get here."

"Cool! Make sure you call me while you there and let me know how everything goes."

"I will and enjoy your night with Cameron. I hope he gives you the best surprise of your life."

"Me too...thanks and talk to you soon!"

I lay back on my bed for a few minutes looking up at the ceiling with the biggest smile on my face. It amazed me that less than an hour ago I was ill to my stomach and ready to lock myself in my room for at least the next week. Now I had breathed in new life and my optimism was in full swing. If all went well, this trip would put Blair and me a step closer on our path to greatness.

Blair

"I feel horrible."

"Blair, we're gonna catch this flight and get you there in time. What more do you want me to do?"

"No, I mean I really feel horrible. My head hurts my stomach is queasy and I need an energy boost. I feel like shit. Tell me you have something that will make me feel better."

"No miracle pill for that. Some coke would boost your energy but I don't want you messing wit' that. But here," Skee said opening a drawer on the nightstand. "Take this B-12 vitamin and I'ma go downstairs and get you some orange juice and fruit. That will help some."

"I'll try whatever because this comedown is not what I need right now." While Skee was downstairs I decided to look in the drawer he got the B-12 from. I wasn't buying that there wasn't something else I could take that would instantly make me feel better. When I opened the drawer all I saw was more vitamins, some other prescription drugs and a small vial of a powered white substance that I assumed was coke. I decided to take that with me in case I got desperate and needed that energy boost. I didn't want to go to my audition with all my energy depleted. Best case scenario the B-12 vitamin would do what it needed and after I put some food on my stomach I would even take a couple caffeine based over-the-counter headache medicine. If all that did the trick then great if not at least I had a backup plan with this coke. Skee already confirmed that it would give me the energy boost I needed, so I had all my bases covered either way.

I caught a glimpse of my reflection in the mirror after shutting the drawer and my face was screaming for some Visine and eye cream. I quickly put on my sunglasses and promised myself that no matter what, once we got to LA I was going straight to my hotel room and going to bed. If I could squeeze a facial in, first thing in the morning, before the audition, that would be perfection. While it was on my mind, I sent Kennedy a text asking her to call our hotel and try to hook it up. In the middle of me texting I heard Skee coming up the stairs so I hastily grabbed my purse and dropped the vial of coke inside before he could see it.

"Here eat this fruit before we go." Skee handed me a bowl of fresh cut peaches, strawberries, mango, melon, apples and grapes. Chewing down and swallowing the healthy food instantly seemed to smooth my insides. Washing it down with orange juice was the perfect touch.

"Thank you. You always seem to give me precisely what I need."

"I take it you're ready to go?"

"Ready as I'll ever be. Besides I've stressed Kennedy out enough for one day. Let's go pick her up before she thinks I've flaked out again and sends out a search team to bring me in. I gave the room one last quick examination before heading out the door.

♥

"So this is what it's like being on a private jet," Kennedy commented when we stepped aboard the Gulfstream G550. "Have to hand it to you, Skee, you know how to travel in style."

"I work hard so I think I at least deserve some reliable transportation." We all laughed in unison at Skee's comment. "Feel free to seat anywhere you like. There are four living areas."

"Thanks, I appreciate that."

"Hello, I'm Katherine and I'll be serving you on this flight. Would you like a drink once you get settled?"

"No I'm good for now."

"If you change your mind let me know as it will be my pleasure to serve on your flight to Los Angeles. I will also bring you a menu shortly, so you can select what you'll be having for dinner tonight."

"Many thanks. I can so get used to this," Kennedy grinned before heading towards the back of the jet.

Before long we were all settled in our seats and had reached a cruising altitude. Being on a private plane with a small amount of people and carte blanche service would beyond spoil you and make you never want to fly commercial again. This was my first time and I was already dreading the day. But if all went well, my life could one day be filled with movie premiers, walking red carpets and private jets.

"What you smiling 'bout over there?" Skee asked taking my hand.

"How this is living the life. It can't possibly get any better."

"If you keep spending time with me, I guarantee you it can."

"It must be an amazing feeling to have the world at your fingertips."

"At first but the more you get the more you want. Then that want feels more like a need. It's never enough."

"While you're trying, the ride must be phenomenal."

"It is and I'm always coming up with new ways to motivate me so that the ride never ends."

"This audition in LA is the beginning of my ride and I'm glad you came with me to share it."

"Me too. I want us to take many more rides together, Blair."

With those words I closed my eyes and began imagining the world my ride would take me on. I envisioned having it all and I would. I mean isn't that what being a Baller Bitch is all about...

Diamond

While I was getting dressed, there were two things constantly on my mind: how was Kennedy and Blair's flight to LA going and what was Cameron's surprise for me tonight. I decided to put those thoughts to left and instead focus on looking extra beautiful tonight, like Cameron had requested.

Following a hunch, I stopped at one of my favorite boutiques in Soho, before I went home. I had this feeling the perfect outfit to wear tonight was waiting for me, and I was right. They had just got a new shipment in a few days earlier and the sales lady was putting the clothes out. That's when I saw the most amazing backless red Miu Miu dress. It had this understated simplicity but at the same time, with the right amount of curves, it would ooze sex appeal. When I peeped the monstrous price tag, I hesitated with the purchase, but I quickly changed my mind when I imagined how great the sex would be, once Cameron ripped it off my body.

As I twirled around in front of the floor length mirror, I knew I had made the right decision. While getting caught up, feeling like Cinder fuckin' rella, I barely heard my cell phone vibrating. I noticed Cameron's name flash on the screen and a smile instantly spread across my face.

"Hi, Baby," I gushed when I answered.

"Hey, beautiful. You just about ready?"

"Yeah, almost."

"How much longer do you need?"

"Ten minutes."

"I'll be out front in twenty."

"You know me so well," I laughed before hanging up. In a lot ways, Cameron did know me so well. I felt like we were perfect for each other. I fucked with my share of low lives before meeting him, but I looked at it as: How would I have known that I had found my Prince, if I hadn't kissed so many frogs?

I brushed a little more translucent powder on my face, applied my favorite matte red lipstick (RiRi Woo by Mac), slipped on a pair of Fifi Spikes, grabbed my purse, and hit the door. The entire time I was going down the elevator, I kept checking my reflection and I had to admit that this was probably the best I had ever looked in my life. Even better than the coming out party I gave myself after I lost all my baby weight and got my body right, then dumped Rico's trifling ass.

When the elevator doors opened, the first I noticed was an array of rose pedals going through the lobby and leading to the front entrance. Standing there was a man dressed in a black suit and tie, holding the door open. As I walked slowly, not sure what was going on, I noticed the concierge and other people who lived in the building standing around smiling at me. I began to feel self-conscious because I couldn't believe this was for me.

"Mr. Robinson has been anticipating your arrival and I must say, you are more than worth the wait," the man holding the door open said, with a gracious smile.

My eyes lit up when I walked outside and the all-white Horse-Drawn Carriage, with Cameron already sitting inside, greeted me. The coachman got out and held my hand as I stepped inside the carriage. My evening was starting off as a fantasy come true and I could only imagine how it was going to end.

"I see you more than delivered on me asking you to look extra beautiful tonight," Cameron commented, before leaning over and giving me a kiss.

"I'm glad you approve but what is all this? Did I forget it was my birthday or something?" I asked jokingly, knowing my birthday was not even close on the calendar.

"Just sit back and enjoy the ride," Cameron said, as the coachman took off slowly. I had no idea where he was taking us but I was certainly looking forward to our final destination.

Kennedy

"We won't have enough time for you to get a massage in the morning, so I made a reservation for tonight," I informed Blair, after we got settled in our hotel rooms.

"I was hoping I could go straight to bed but a massage does sound good right about now."

"The spa is right in the hotel, so once you're done you can go back to your room and get some sleep."

'True. Let me get myself together and I'll go down there in a few."

"Wise decision. I want you to be relaxed and feel your best at the audition."

"Do you think they'll be able to squeeze in a facial? My face is in critical need of a lil' rehabilitation."

"I'm sure that won't be a problem. I'll call them now and add that to your services. Do you want me to add anything else?"

"Whatever you can think of that will help contribute to me looking and feeling like a superstar tomorrow."

"Got it, but Blair, don't stress yourself over the audition. You're going to do great. Just show up and give it your best. No matter what happens..."

"The only thing that's going to happen is I'm walking away with the part," Blair stated adamantly, cutting me off.

"I want you to get the part, too, but for some reason if you don't, there will be other auditions."

"Not like this. This role is a game changer and I have to nail it."

I couldn't argue with Blair about that. If she were able to snag this role, it would have a major impact on her career. It had the potential to make her the new 'it' girl in Hollywood. With that being the case, I still didn't want Blair to give up her hopes and dreams of becoming a movie star if she didn't land the part. Just the fact she was being considered and able to audition was a huge feat in itself, especially with her being a newcomer.

"And you will nail it," I said, wanting to encourage her. As beautiful and talented as Blair was, I had picked up that she had a lot of insecurities. In this business, having confidence meant a lot and I needed Blair to tap into all of hers.

"Thanks, Kennedy, I needed to hear that from you. You never hold back when it comes to speaking the truth about business, so you saying that--it means a lot to me."

"And I meant every word. Oh, I forgot to tell you that I had my stylist friend pull the perfect dress for you to wear to the audition tomorrow."

"Really? I brought something to wear but if you think what you have would work better then I'll definitely take a look."

"Trust me, this dress has Grad school mistress of

the President written on the designer tag. Not only are you going to turn everyone's head when you walk in but it has the character you're playing written all over it. The director will swear you're Liza."

"Wow can't wait to see it."

"Just hit me up when you're done at the spa and I'll drop if off at your room."

"Can you come drop it off now? I think once I'm finished with my massage I'll be so tired that once I hit my room, I'm passing out on the bed."

"I feel you. Only thing is I ordered some room service and they'll probably be here any minute."

"No problem. Once you're done eating, drop it off then. Skee will be here. I'll let him know to be expecting you."

"Cool. Enjoy being pampered and of course, call me if you need me. If I don't hear from you, I'll see you in the morning."

"Thanks!"

After devouring my steak and french fries, I headed upstairs to drop off Blair's dress. It seemed to be taking forever for Skee to come to the door but right when I was about to turn and leave, I heard the knob turning.

"Hey, I hope I didn't disturb you. I was coming to drop off Blair's dress," I said, reaching out to hand it to Skee.

"You're not disturbing me, come in." Before I could tell him that wouldn't be necessary, he had started walking off and the door was about to shut in my face.

"You can leave it on the chair," he said, walking towards the bar.

Once I got inside their suite, I realized why it took Skee so long to answer. Their room was more than triple my size. I figured it was the Presidential Suite or something. There was glass, marble, and even a staircase that led upstairs. Skee was definitely living that good life. I almost forgot what I came for, because I was too busy drooling over how fab their suite was, but quickly gathered my thoughts. Without saying another word I placed the dress on the chair and headed back towards the door.

"What are Blair's chances of getting that role?" I heard Skee ask, right before I turned the doorknob to leave.

"I think they're pretty good. I mean the fact she's here for an audition means a lot."

"Maybe, or it could be just that...an audition." I raised an eyebrow wondering where Skee was going with this conversation. "I'm going on tour in a few months and I want Blair to come with me."

"You'll have to take that up with Blair."

"Well, if she doesn't get the part, then I won't have to worry about it."

"Are you saying that you don't want Blair to get the role?"

"Not if it's going to interfere with the plans I have for her."

"And those plans would be what...her trailing behind you, while you continue to live out your dreams and she puts hers on hold?"

"Blair being able to travel the world with me hardly equates to her putting her dreams on hold."

"Let me ask you a question: If you don't want Blair to get the part, why did you let us use your private jet to get here?"

"Because I care about Blair and if I can help her, I will."

"If you want to be helpful, then support her career choice, which is to be an actress, not your arm candy."

"Even if Blair gets this role, it won't provide her the type of money to live the lifestyle I can give her. We both know there isn't any stability in that business."

"I'm sure people told you the same thing when you were trying to break into the music industry. Now look at you, private planes, worldwide tours with sold out arenas, and Penthouse Suites like this," I said, looking around. "Just think, if you had listened to the naysayers, none of this would be yours."

"Yeah, I beat the odds but those odds are stacked even higher against Blair."

"You might be right, but just like you beat the odds, I believe Blair will, too." Skee was now sitting down in the living room area, with a drink in one hand and the TV remote control in the other. I could hear the ice shifting in his glass. He was so full of himself and all I could think was *if only a tad of Skee's confidence rubbed off on Blair, she would kick ass on every audition she went on.*

"Thanks for the convo but you can go now. We'll see you in the morning." Skee kept his eyes glued to the television, while basically throwing me out. I didn't mind because I was ready to go, but he did have my insides burning up. Skee was another Michael but I thought he might be worse. Blair knew exactly what she was getting when dealing with him, but Skee had a much more subtle approach with his controlling ways. He dangled all the trappings of success in front of Blair's eyes, hoping it would be so tempting she wouldn't be able to resist-- and most women wouldn't. The problem with that was Skee held the power because it all belonged to him. I only hoped that Blair would realize selling her soul to Skee for a moment of happiness wasn't worth it, when she could have a lifetime of independence.

Blair

When I stared at myself in the mirror, panic struck me. Today was the moment of truth, either put up or shut up, and deep down inside I wasn't sure if I had the necessary talent to deliver. So much uncertainty consumed me and I hated myself for feeling this way. I thought about Michael and how he always told me I didn't have what it took to make it in the industry. I thought about my mother, growing up and nobody ever wanting me. I never seemed to be good enough and I was petrified that I was about to prove all of them right. I reached for my purse and slowly opened it up. I unzipped the small compartment and pulled out the vile of cocaine. I thought if I sniffed one line it could give me the self-confidence boost I was in dire need of. I looked down at the coke and then my reflection in the mirror.

"Blair, you're stronger than this. You don't need a drug to nail your audition. You have what it takes, you just have to believe that." As I said those words out loud, I was waiting for them to sink into my spirit, so I could believe them myself. As all these thoughts played in my mind, I then saw that Kennedy was calling.

"Hello."

"It's time to go. We can't be late. I'm downstairs and the car is waiting for us."

"I'm on my way. Just give me a couple more minutes."

"Okay, but hurry."

When I hung up with Kennedy, I took a few deep breaths. I glanced back down at the cocaine that seemed to be calling my name. The pure white powder seemed almost harmless. I brushed my hair one last time, adjusted my clothes, tossed the cocaine back in my purse, and walked out the bathroom.

"Kennedy just called. The car is downstairs. Are you ready to go?"

"The question is: are *you* ready?"

I wasn't sure how to answer Skee's question.

"Ready as I'll ever be," I replied as we left our hotel room. There was complete silence until we reached the awaiting SUV.

"I knew that dress would look perfect on you when I first laid eyes on it!" Kennedy screamed in excitement. "You are Liza," she declared.

"Thank you," I blushed. I had to admit Kennedy's excitement over my appearance was exactly what I needed to make me feel a little more self-assured. Her enthusiasm had quickly rubbed off on me. I couldn't lie: the bright, yellow Alexander McQueen dress I was wearing did scream subtle seductress.

"Skee, doesn't Blair look absolutely stunning," Kennedy stated. I felt some sort of weird vibe but brushed it off.

"She always does," he responded, gently rubbing my upper thigh.

"I'm glad you both think I look great, but let's hope the audition goes well."

"Blair, it's only natural for you to be nervous, but try to relax. Do you know your lines?"

"Of course, I've practiced them enough."

"Practice is always good. You want to be prepared, but don't worry about memorizing the lines. Focus on encompassing the personality of the character, with a touch of your own natural charm."

"That's excellent advice...thank you."

"You're welcome. I'm here to support you and be your biggest cheerleader.

"It's great to finally see both of you again," Marcus smiled when we walked into the studio where the auditions were being held.

"It's good to see you, too, and thank you for giving me this opportunity."

"Yes, we both appreciate it," Kennedy added.

"Listen, like I told you, when I came across this part, I thought of you, Blair. Are you ready? Because they're waiting for you."

"Yes, I'm ready."

"Then follow me," Marcus said, about to lead the way.

"I'll be out here waiting for you, Blair. You're going to do great!"

"Thank you, Kennedy. I mean that. Thank you for

believing in me when I didn't even believe in myself."

"Girl, stop! Don't make me tear up in here and you damn sure can't tear up. I can't have you messing up your makeup, now go." We both laughed as if to stop ourselves from crying. I turned and continued to follow Marcus to the door, with Skee by my side.

"I'll be out shortly, keep your fingers crossed for me," I smiled.

"I'm coming inside with you, while you do your audition."

"I'm sorry, but I'm going to need you to wait out here. It's a closed audition," Marcus informed Skee.

"I'm Skee Patron. I'm sure nobody will have a problem with me going inside and watching my girlfriend's audition."

"Like I said, it's a closed audition."

"Baby, relax. I'll be out shortly. You can wait out here and keep Kennedy company."

"I don't want to stay out here with Kennedy. I want to come inside with you."

"Is there a problem?" Kennedy walked up to us and asked casually.

"I was explaining that no one is allowed inside for the audition, but Blair," stated Marcus, clearly becoming annoyed.

"Sounds reasonable to me. So, what's the problem?"

"I want to go inside with Blair, and watch her audition," Skee said, not backing down.

"Skee, please wait out here with Kennedy. I'm already nervous. I don't need any unnecessary confusion. I'll be out shortly," I said, kissing him on the cheek. "I'm ready, Marcus. Lets go."

When I entered the room I heard the doors slam behind me. I turned around for a brief second, in the direction I heard the noise, and then I focused my attention back on the five faces staring at me. I fought through my anxiety and managed to conjure up one of those beauty pageant smiles. *It's all or nothing, Kennedy... time to kick ass.*

Diamond

After the horse-drawn carriage took Cameron and I for a romantic ride through Central Park, we finally stopped at a candle lit dinner that was set up under a gazebo. It was decorated with an assortment of flowers and rose pedals leading to the table for two. There were beautiful chandeliers hanging from trees and an orchestra playing dreamy music. Cameron took my hand and led me to the gazebo.

"Will you dance with me?" Cameron asked, lifting my arm up.

"Of course." When I looked up at Cameron, he had never looked more handsome. His charcoal, grey tailored suit fit his tall, muscular body to perfection.

"Did I tell you how beautiful you look tonight?"

"Yes, several times, but I haven't gotten tired of hearing it," I giggled. "Did I tell you that you're the most handsome man I've ever laid eyes on?"

"Nope, but say it again because it's wonderful for my ego."

"You have an ego...I never would've guessed."

"Not really, but having you as my woman has

probably been my biggest ego booster yet."

"Stop it."

"I'm serious. Everyday I wake up and I wonder: What have I done to deserve a woman that makes me so incredibly happy? I was going to wait until after dinner, but I can't."

"Can't what?" I asked, as Cameron nodded his head, motioning towards one of the men there. A few minutes later, a limo pulled up. The driver opened the passenger door as my mother and daughter stepped out.

"Mommy," Destiny smiled, running towards me. I lifted her up and gave her a kiss, and Cameron kissed her, too. "Hi Cammie," Destiny grinned. I always got such a kick at her calling him that, since she couldn't say Cameron yet.

"Mom, you're here, too. What is going on?"

"You haven't figured it out, yet?" Cameron said, shaking his head with a smirk on his face. "There is no doubt in my mind you are my soulmate," Cameron began, as he got down on bended knee.

"This can't be real," I uttered, with my voice cracking. I felt my entire body shaking, as I saw Cameron pull out the most amazing diamond sparkler I had ever seen. Both my mother and Destiny covered their mouths, as if they were in as much disbelief as me. My mom then took Destiny out of my arms and held her, which made me relieved, because I honestly thought I was about to pass out from shock.

"I never allowed myself to imagine finding a woman I wanted to spend the rest of my life with, because I didn't think it was possible, and then I met you. Your smile had this way of turning my worst days into something magical. When I thought you had been taken from my life, I couldn't envision living one more day without you in it. Not only have you brought me so much happiness, but you've blessed me by bringing your daughter into my life, too. I'm here on bended knee, in front of the people who love you most, asking for your hand in marriage. Diamond O'Toole, will you marry me?"

"Yes! Yes! Yes! I will marry you!" I wanted to scream a million times. When Cameron slid the ring on my finger, unable to holdback, all these tears rushed out of me.

"Mommy, what's wrong? Don't cry," Destiny said, leaning her head on my shoulder.

"These are tears of happiness, baby. Cammie has made your mommy the happiest girl in the whole wide world."

"We love you, Cammie," Destiny smiled and said.

"I love you, too," Cameron smiled back, taking Destiny from my mom and holding her high in the air, like she loved so much.

I had been so caught up in Cameron's elaborate proposal that I didn't even realize he had a photographer and a videographer capturing every moment. Now, we would always be able to reflect on this time and share it with the child I hoped we would have together, one day.

When I opened my eyes the next morning, at first I

thought last night was all a dream, until the diamond decorating my finger reminded me this was my reality. I immediately turned towards Cameron's side of the bed and to my disappointment, he wasn't there. Instead, there was a handwritten note with a long stem rose:

Good morning Beautiful,

I wish, when you woke up, that I was right there holding you in my arms, but I had to make the team flight. I'll be back in a few days but I'll call you, once I get settled in my hotel room. In case you didn't know, last night you made me the happiest man in the world. I'm looking forward to letting everyone know that you're now my fiancée and very soon, you'll be my wife. I love you.

Cameron

I think I re-read the note about one hundred times and each time felt like the first. One thing Cameron was right about: I hated not being in his arms when I woke up, but it was the playoffs and I knew how much getting a ring meant to him, so I could be patient for a few days, until he returned. I went back to admiring my diamond engagement ring, until my cell phone ringing interrupted me. I didn't recognize the number but decided to answer anyway. Quickly, I realized that was a mistake.

"Hello."

"Destiny just told me she's gettin' a new daddy.

What the fuck is that shit about?"

"Rico, I hope you ain't cursing like that in front of our daughter?" I huffed. Mad at myself for answering the phone.

"My mom took Destiny to the park, so, she's not hearing any of this, but back to my question. Don't be tryna' get that basketball nigga to replace me in my daughter's life. She got one daddy and that's me. Plus, that relationship ain't gon' last anyway. I give ya' 'bout two more months and that nigga gon' cash yo' ass in for the next gold-digging trick."

"First of all, ain't nobody tryna' replace you. Cameron loves Destiny, and they have gotten closer, which is natural since he's my man. My fault, I meant fiancé," I snapped, smiling at the rock on my finger.

"Yo' fiancé! Bitch, please, that nigga ain't marrying you! Stop lyin' on this motherfuckin' phone."

"Nigga, ain't nobody lying. Don't be mad 'cause I got a real man in my life who wants to make me his wife."

"What, you trapped him? You got pregnant, so now the nigga gon' marry you? I knew you was a scandalous ass gold-digger."

"No, I'm not pregnant. Cameron and I are very much in love. And when we do decide to have a baby it won't be any of your business. You need to focus on being a father to our daughter and don't worry about what's going on with my uterus. Now, unless you have something else to discuss regarding Destiny, this conversation is over," I said, and ended the call without waiting to hear his reply.

Rico had my blood pressure rising. Not only did this clown want to come at me, regarding my relationship with Cameron, but he also set me up. I thought about the last words Parish spoke before I put a bullet in his head. *I'ma die wit' a smile on my face knowing yo' own baby daddy set you up to be robbed. He even gave me permission to smash the pussy.* I hated that this nigga had fucked up my morning with that bullshit phone call, but it made me come to the realization I needed to get rid of Rico, ASAP. He had been a thorn in my side long enough.

Kennedy

"Congrats! Girl, I'm so proud of you," I beamed as we held up our champagne glasses.

"Kennedy, Your congratulations are a bit premature. We don't know if I got the part yet."

"It doesn't matter, we still have a lot to celebrate. You had your first audition with a major movie studio. That's huge! And lets not forget, Marcus said you were fantastic. Those were his exact words."

"Yeah, he did say that," Blair blushed, fidgeting in her chair.

"So, no matter what happened, you gave a great audition in front of major players, in Hollywood. Even if you don't get this part, they will remember you when something else comes up. So, be proud of yourself. You were nervous but you still showed up and delivered."

"Kennedy, I don't know what I would do without you. You are such a great cheerleader and I appreciate it more than you know."

"Are you ready to go? I told this producer I was in town for a couple days and he wanted me to listen to some tracks I might use for my next CD," Skee said.

"Oh, I wanted to hangout with Kennedy for a little longer. Why don't you go meet up with the producer and we can see each other later on."

"That doesn't work for me," Skee stated. The look in Skee's eyes was somewhat unnerving. He didn't raise his voice or anything but his vibe wasn't right.

"Blair, I'll be fine. Go with Skee and we can meet up later for dinner," I said, wanting to cease any potential confrontation.

"Are you sure? Or if you want, you can come with us."

"No, I'm good. We'll hook up later on."

"Okay, I'll call you--and Kennedy, thanks again, for everything," Blair smiled, giving me a hug and a kiss on the cheek, before walking off with Skee. Right when I started shaking my head thinking about the two of them, I felt my purse vibrating. I reached inside and grabbed my phone.

"Hey, Diamond!"

"You all must be having a great time because I haven't heard a peep out of you."

"More like super busy. I swear I was about to call you to vent about this damn Skee, but as if you were reading my mind, you called first."

"Do tell, what happened with Skee?"

"Girl, where do I start? First, when I went to drop off Blair's dress, he basically told me that he hoped Blair didn't get the part, so she could travel with him on his upcoming world tour. Then, I felt he was purposely trying to sabotage her audition by insisting on going in with her. It was crazy."

"What! He sounds like another Michael."

"Yeah, but in my opinion he might be worse. We were having drinks, celebrating Blair's audition, and he shut it down saying he needed to go meet with some producer. Blair wanted to stay with me but I thought he was going to throw a temper tantrum like a four-year-old, so I told Blair we could meet up for dinner later."

"Girl, stop!"

"I'm serious. Skee wants Blair to revolve her life around him. I wonder what he's going to do, once he realizes she's going to have a career of her own."

"Speaking of Blair's career, how did her audition go?"

"We weren't allowed in the room, but Marcus said she did great."

"Yes! Yes! That's my girl!" Diamond belted.

"I know. I'm so proud of her."

"So, when will you find out if she got the part?"

"Soon, I hope. Marcus didn't give me a definitive date, but he said they are trying to cast the part as soon as possible, because they've already been green lit to start filming."

"Wow! I'm keeping my fingers crossed. I'm ready to see Blair on the big screen."

"Me too, but I won't be sitting around, twiddling my thumbs, waiting to see if she gets the part. I'm going to continue to keep Blair's name on the blogs and in the media. The more people see her face and name, the better."

"That sounds like a plan to me."

"So, what's going on with you?"

"I have some exciting news!"

"Do tell."

"When are you all coming back?"

"Tomorrow morning. Hopefully Skee will let me back on the jet," I giggled.

"He won't do you like that but just in case, you got airfare? If not, I can Western Union you some coins." We both burst out laughing. "But real talk, the three of us need to get together tomorrow night for dinner and drinks."

"So, I have to wait until then to hear your exciting news?"

"Yes, but I promise you it'll be worth the wait. Now, let me get off this phone, 'cause I'm already late for my hair appointment. See you ladies tomorrow night!"

When I got off the phone with Diamond, I started wondering what her exciting news was. Different scenarios played in my head and once again, the vibration of my cell phone interrupted my thoughts. I instantly got excited when I realized it was Marcus.

"Hi, Marcus! I wasn't expecting to hear from you so soon. Has a decision already been made?"

"Not yet. I was actually calling about something else."

"You sound serious. What is it?"

"Beyond our professional relationship, you also know that I like how you move, your drive, and how you conduct yourself while handling business." As Marcus was talking, I gave my phone the side eye, wondering was this some sort of awkward way of Marcus letting me know he was interested in me, but I quickly brushed that off, since he didn't seem like the type that would mix business and pleasure.

"Thank you," I said, not able to come up with anything else, since I had no clue where he was going with this conversation.

"For those reasons, I wanted to put you on alert that Darcy Woods is trying to blacklist you in this business."

"What! You have to be kidding me!" I yelled. When I noticed everyone in the restaurant turned around to see who the crazy person yelling on the phone was, I instantly lowered my voice. I then took a big gulp of my champagne, trying to calm my nerves. I signaled the waiter to bring me over another.

"I didn't want to upset you, especially after how great things went with Blair this morning, but I had to warn you. Darcy knows a lot of people in this industry and to some, her word holds a lot of weight."

"This isn't going to affect Blair's chances of getting the part, is it?" I asked, starting to panic.

"Calm down. This won't have any effect on Blair's audition, but it is causing a problem with that PR job I offered you."

"Why? I thought the account was basically mine, if I accepted it."

"In my mind it was. When I brought it up to my partner, he revealed to me that Darcy told him she fired you, after discovering you were stealing money from the company."

"That's a lie!"

"I've known you for some time now and when my

partner brought it up to me that was my first reaction, but he's a fan of Darcy's work. From what I understand, she put together a huge charity event for Tyler Blake and he was very impressed."

"I did that event from start to finish. All Darcy did was show up on the red carpet to have her picture taken. But of course, she gets all the credit."

"So, what now? I'm out of the running to get the account?"

"He wants to give Darcy the account, but I'm still pushing for you. We have a third partner and his vote will be the deciding factor."

"Marcus, you have to believe that I never stole from Darcy. She's lying. I worked my butt off for her and all she wanted to do was give me peanuts. She never gave me commissions I was due but wanted me to be her personal slave. I had enough and wanted to branch out on my own. Darcy is spreading these vicious lies because she doesn't want to see me prosper."

"Kennedy, I hope what I shared doesn't discourage you, but instead motivates you to work harder to accomplish what you want. I have to take another call but I'll be in touch. Try to stay positive. Bye."

"Bye," I managed to say, although I was ready to break my cell into a million pieces.

Darcy had truly crossed the line this time. It was one thing for her to fuck me over when I worked for her, but now she was trying to keep me from making a living. This time she wouldn't get away with it, though. I planned on serving Darcy Woods a lesson she would never forget, I thought, as I sipped on my glass of champagne.

Blair

"So, what did you think about the tracks?" I asked Skee, as we rode in the back of the chauffer-driven SUV.

"They were a'ight. It's the same type of beats everybody's using right now. I'm looking for a new and different sound for my upcoming CD. That shit wasn't it, but I'm not stressed. I'll find the sound I'm looking for. It might come from a super producer or it might come from some young, unknown kid who's never had a hit. I don't care where it comes from, as long as I get it."

"I'm sure you will. You always get what you want."

"You think so?"

"Of course," I laughed, thinking Skee's question was silly.

"So, that means you're mine, all mine?"

"Is that what you want for me, to be yours?"

"What do you think?"

"I love being with you and I think you enjoy being with me, too, but you've been a superstar for a while now, so I'm sure you've had lots of women you've enjoyed being with."

"You're right, the last few years of my life has been

an endless assortment of women. Some I've enjoyed more than others but none of them I've wanted to keep, until you."

"Hmmm, why don't I believe you?"

"I don't know. For the last few months, we've been together almost everyday and I never get tired of you. That's huge for me."

"Oh, so normally you get tired of women quickly and toss them to the side?"

"Basically," Skee nodded.

"You're the worst," I laughed, hitting him on the arm.

"You said it, I was just telling the truth."

"Sometimes I forget how blatantly honest you are."

"I'm honest and direct. I want you to be mine. There's something special about you."

"Really?"

"Yes," Skee said, stroking the side of my face.

"I do feel special when I'm with you."

Skee leaned over and kissed me, and his lips always felt magical to me. The kisses became more intense and I was ready to get naked in the back of the SUV.

"Lets go shopping."

"Where the hell did that come from? We're kissing and you bring up going shopping."

"I thought all women liked to go shopping."

"Yeah, but while kissing you, shopping was the furthest thing on my mind. I was thinking we could go back to our hotel room."

"And we will, after we go shopping. I want to make sure you have everything you need for my tour."

"We're not even sure if I'll be able to go on tour

with you. What if I get the part, which I'm keeping my fingers crossed that I do."

"It's always good to be prepared, just in case. Now, lets go shopping."

Skee and I spent the next few hours hitting store after store, on Rodeo Drive, until we ended up at Maxfield LA, on 8825 Melrose Avenue, in West Hollywood.

"This place looks more like an art gallery or a museum," I commented, when Skee and I were going inside the store.

"Yep, but they have the latest and hottest of everything up in here. They also get exclusive shit from all over the world that nobody else has but them."

"Mr. Patron, it's good to see you again," a lady with a foreign accent said, when we came in. "You should've called me, I would've had everything prepared for you."

"It was a last minute decision."

"No problem. I'll get everything ready for you now."

"This time I'm not here for myself. It's for my beautiful woman, Blair."

"She is a beauty," the lady smiled, clearly used to kissing Skee's ass and enjoying doing so. "Blair, it will be our pleasure to serve you. Mr. Patron is one of our best customers."

"Thank you."

"Follow me." The lady led us over to a private sitting area. After we sat down, some glasses, champagne, and water were brought out. Once we were settled, the staff began bringing out some of he most amazing clothes I had ever seen. Brands like Mastermind Japan, Roland Mouret, Carol Christian Poella, and Balmain.

"I love that dress right there," I remarked, pointing to a cream Celine dress.

"It's okay," Skee countered, basically rejecting my choice. "But that one, is going to look unbelievable on you," he said nodding his head at a red Chanel outfit. At this point Skee's dismissive attitude didn't even bother me. I was used to it. I might've picked out one pair of earrings during our entire shopping spree. Everything else was Skee's choice. It was as if he dressed me to be his personal muse. But being with Skee always felt like the ultimate high, so I willingly let him lead the way, and I relished every minute of it.

Diamond

"I wish Kennedy would hurry up. We have so much to talk about today," I gushed to Blair. I made sure not to be too animated with my hand gestures, because I didn't want to share my engagement news until Kennedy got here.

"Kennedy is normally so punctual and I'm the late one, so this is odd. Let me call her again."

"Don't bother, here she comes now," I said, waving my hand.

"Hey ladies! I apologize for being late, but I was handling some very important business."

"Do share. The way your eyes lit up, it sounds very important."

"Did you speak to Marcus? Did he tell you if I got the role or not?"

"Not yet, Blair. But I'm sure we'll be hearing something soon. Like I told you, they're anxious to start filming."

"Maybe that means they already picked the actress and it's not me."

"Girl, if you don't stop being a Debbie Downer," I

said, reaching across the table and slapping Blair on the arm. I instantly regretted my reflex action.

"What the fuck did I just see flash across this table, almost blinding me!"

"Huh, what are you talking about," I mumbled, trying to play it off.

"Don't "huh" me! Give me your hand," Kennedy demanded.

I huffed for a second, and then glanced at Kennedy then Blair. "Dammit! I wanted to wait until after the waitress brought the champagne to share the news. But of course, I ruined it, trying to slap some sense into Blair."

"Oh, so now it's my fault? Don't blame me for your violent temper," Blair laughed. "But seriously, before we scream at the top of our lungs, is the news you want to share what I think it is?"

I held up my hand and wiggled my fingers. "I guess Cameron likes it, 'cause he put a ring on it.'"

"Ahhhhhhh!" Kennedy and Blair belted out at the same time, waving their arms. Then they got out of their chairs and hugged me.

"This is so amazing you're going to make me cry," Blair snuffled.

"Girl, sit back down. I haven't even told you how Cameron proposed. It's so sweet. Now *that's* gonna make you cry."

"Let me see that ring again," Kennedy said, cradling my hand. "Wow! Girl, this is a minimum of ten carats on your finger."

"I think you're right. It's huge but it looks very

classy," Blair added. "So, tell us how he proposed."

As I gave the play by play of how Cameron proposed, I felt I was reliving it all over again and by the time I was finished, all three of us were watery eyed. If I hadn't been there, I wouldn't believe such a fairytale story. Not only that, even looking at the ring it was still hard for me to accept I was the star of that fairytale.

"That was amazing, Diamond. It was such an inspiring story. It lets you know that true love still exists."

"Blair, you're such a hopeless romantic. You've been that way since we were little girls."

"You're right. I just hope I find my prince soon or maybe I already have," Blair smiled. "But this isn't about me. This is your moment and you have, and I'm so happy for you. I can't wait for us to start planning the wedding!"

"I know but I'm not in a big rush. I'm going to wait for this playoff season to end, before I even start asking Cameron about a date."

"I'm surprised you're not on the road with him for the away games."

"I would've but I had to meet with my attorney earlier today about that case."

"How did it go? I thought the charges were supposed to be dismissed."

"It's not that simple. I mean, my attorney does believe the charges will be dropped because supposedly, some of the prosecution witnesses have disappeared but you know the court system never wants to make things easy for you. I'm not worried, though. My attorney is much more optimistic now and so am I. So optimistic, that I'm ready to go full blast on our business venture, Kennedy."

"Really!?"

"Yes! Instead of being a silent partner, I want to be all in the mix, too. Of course, after I get this court bullshit behind me, but I think it's going to happen within the next few weeks. The soon-to-be Mrs. Cameron Robinson needs to have a respectable career. So, I'm going to spend a lot of moolah promoting us."

"Girl, you are getting me extra excited! I'm so honored and lucky to have you as a partner. Hopefully, I can get a few things under control quickly, because if I do there's no stopping us and our company will be a huge success."

"A few things like what?" I inquired. "It seems like everything has been coming along great. Besides what you've been doing for Blair, you also have that contract that Marcus offered you, for their new business."

"Yeah, that was before Darcy started spreading her vicious lies."

"Get the fuck outta here! What is that witch up to now?"

"She told Marcus' business partner that she fired me because I was stealing from the company."

"You can't be serious," I said, shaking my head.

"Did you tell him the real reason she fired you was because she wanted you to dump me as a client, because of her relationship with Michael?"

"Blair, I didn't even want to give Marcus the Young and the Restless version. There is no need to get him caught up in that soap opera. He doesn't need to know about your personal life. I did tell him it was a lie, which he pretty much knew anyway."

"So, then what's the problem? Why is he trying to renege on the gig?"

"It's not him; it's one of his partners. He's cool with Darcy and she lied and told him she put together that fabulous charity event that I busted my ass on, so he wants to give the account to her."

"This is some straight bullshit," I huffed, crossing my arms in disgust.

"No worries. I got something brewing for Ms. Darcy Woods. She wants to spread lies on me but when she gets hit with the truth, all hell is gonna break loose."

"Huh? You have some dirt on Darcy?" Blair questioned, leaning forward in her chair.

"Sure do and it's juicy."

"You better spill," I popped.

"Check it. Around that time when Darcy didn't pay me my bonus, because she claimed she was having financial issues, of course I thought she was lying. So, I began snooping around, eavesdropping--you know, sneaky shit," Kennedy laughed, as she high-fived us.

"What did you find out?" Blair and I both asked at the same time.

"Darcy is only the owner of her PR firm on paper. It's actually funded by some notorious drug dealer, who is using it to launder money."

"Get out!" Blair's eyes widened.

"Yes and I have proof. I've been holding onto it for months, so I could have leverage over Darcy for reasons just like this one."

"You're going to threaten Darcy with it?"

"Nope. I'm going to send all the information to a friend of mine at the New York Post. I'm going to have them first run a blind item as a teaser and then have them do a full fledge article exposing Darcy and all of her dirty little secrets. But of course, I'll remain an anonymous source."

"That will teach her to fuck with you. Sounds like a great idea to me, Kennedy," I declared, winking my eye at her.

"Yeah, me too! If only I could be a fly on the wall when she opens up the paper."

"I'm glad I won't be, because I don't want to be around when Darcy explodes. Talk about shit hitting the fan. Darcy is gonna tear that entire office up. Ha!"

"She deserves it. She should've never fucked with you. You were the best employee she ever had and all she did was take you for granted."

"And treated me like shit. But she's going to pay and it's going to cost her more than just her business. Once this story breaks and law enforcement gets wind of it, Darcy and the real owner of her company are going to be looking at jail time, and a lot of it."

"I never thought about that, but you're right," Blair said. "Do you know who the owner is?"

"Of course. I mean, I don't know him personally, but it's some guy named Renny O'Neal. He's supposed to be some huge Drug Kingpin. Luckily for me, he'll never know that it was me that exposed him and his illegal shenanigans. Honestly, he's just a causality of Darcy's payback, but again, it's not my problem. She should've left me the fuck alone. Diamond, are you okay?" Kennedy asked, when I started choking on my appetizer.

"Here, drink some water," Blair said, handing me a glass of water.

"Sorry about that. My food went down the wrong way. I'm fine," I lied. When Kennedy said the name Renny O'Neal, I almost fell out of my chair. "So, when are you planning on moving forward with this?"

"Pronto. That's why I was late. I was meeting with my contact at the Post. He is ready to get this ball rolling ASAP. He seems more excited about breaking this story than me. He thinks it's going to garner him a bunch of praise and prestige as a *real* journalist."

As Blair continued to throw one question after another to Kennedy, acting like a little girl in a classroom enthralled by what she was learning from her teacher, I felt like I wanted to vomit. There was no way I could let Kennedy drop this bomb to the New York Post, or anybody else. Not only had Renny saved my life, but he had also been my connect. I was already on the watch list for the police, if this shit about Renny got out, there was no doubt I would go down, too.

Kennedy

"Kennedy, I think you should wait before pressing go on this," I said, still trying to come up with an excuse that sounded legitimate.

"Why would I do that?"

"Yeah, why would she do that? I mean, if anybody deserves to go down, it's Darcy. Plus, she's trying to ruin Kennedy's chances of having her own successful business by spreading nasty lies."

"That's true and she needs to be dealt with, but I'm not sure if this is the best way of going about it."

"But you were just cheering me on, why the sudden change?"

"I'll admit, I got caught up in the moment, but now that I'm thinking about it, this could lead to some serious problems for you."

"How?"

"What if it gets out that you leaked this information. That means the police might want to talk to you and it could get back to that drug dealer who actually owns the company. He might be dangerous and try to come at you on some retaliation type shit."

"Diamond, don't you think you're being a little dramatic? You've been watching too many gangster movies."

"Listen, I'm only telling you what could happen."

"First of all, the guy at the Post would never give me up. He would completely ruin his reputation as a journalist and in this business, if he did. And I doubt that Renny dude would want to come at me. If anything, Darcy is going to be the one who needs protection because I'm sure that's who the guy is going to blame."

"You might be absolutely right but it's never good to make emotional decisions. I think you should take a few days to think about this and make sure it's what you really want to do."

"I have thought about it and I'm positive it's what I want to do. If Darcy has already talked shit about me to Marcus's partner, I can only imagine how many other people she's spreading her lies to. This business is very cutthroat as is and I don't need that hussy fucking up our chances of having a successful PR firm."

"I agree with what both of you are saying. Darcy totally deserves everything you're about to throw at her. On the other hand, I've also made so many emotional decisions and they always come back to bite me in the ass. I don't think waiting a few days to make sure it's what you really want to do is going to hurt anything."

"It wouldn't but I can't imagine anything happening that would make me change my mind. Darcy Woods is going down, end of story. I guess waiting a few days to make that happen is doable."

"Kennedy, I think you made a good decision. You

might be completely right and in a couple days you can still decide to release all of your artillery on Darcy, but you could also change your mind because an even better option is presented to you. You just never know what can happen in forty-eight hours."

"I'm glad we were able to get that resolved, now we can move on to the next topic, I think...hold on, I have to take this call," Blair said, picking up her iPhone. "Hey, what's up?"

I wasn't sure who Blair was talking to, but I had an idea based on the smile on her face. I decided right then what our next topic of conversation would be.

"We're at Norma's," I heard Blair say. "What's the address here?"

"119 W 56th Street. Inside the Le Parker Meridien," Diamond said."

"Thanks," Blair mouthed in a low voice and continued her conversation.

"Diamond, I want you to know that I really am excited about us working together and I do respect your opinion."

"Thanks, I sense a "but", though."

"No "but". At first, I did somewhat brush off your suggestion about waiting to burst Darcy's bubble and I shouldn't have done that. Not only are we friends, but we're about to be partners in a business. I need to always take your advice into consideration because I know it comes from a positive place."

"It really does. I only want what's best for you and our company," Diamond smiled.

"Sorry about that," Blair said, getting off her call.

"Let me guess, that was Skee."

"Yeah, he was going to come join us for lunch."

"Blair, this was supposed to be for ladies only lunch. No boyfriends allowed."

"I know Diamond, but I didn't want to be rude. It doesn't matter because while we were on the phone he got a text from his manager. He has to get on this conference call with some sponsors about his upcoming tour. We're going to meet up later."

"Things seem to be getting very serious with you and Skee. Are you all officially a couple now?" Diamond probed.

"Well, according to all the blogs they are."

"You handle my PR. If the blogs are reporting that, isn't it because of you?"

"Blair, I haven't fed information about you and Skee to the media in weeks. All this new stuff is from events, photos, and other outings you all attend together."

'That's a good thing, right? You said you wanted to keep me relevant and my name out there, so being with Skee is doing that."

"I guess, but ultimately I want your relevance to come from your body of work and not from being some rappers girlfriend."

"I think what Kennedy is trying to say is that she wants you to shine on your own and you will," Diamond added, trying to smooth shit over, which honestly I didn't want her to do.

"Listen, Blair, I think you are truly talented and I'm determined," I looked over at Diamond, "I mean we're determined," Diamond cheesed up when I added her to the mix. We are partners and it was time I programmed my brain to start acknowledging that at all times.

"Thank you and yes, we are determined...now continue, Kennedy."

"We're determined to make you a star, but my question is: Do you really want it?"

"Of course, why would you even ask such a silly question?"

"Because unless you're wearing blinders, Skee has no desire for you to be a star in your own right."

"That's not true."

"Yes the hell it is. When we were in LA he basically told me that. He's hoping you don't get the role in this movie, so you can go on tour with him."

"I think you misunderstood him. Skee is very supportive. Remember, if it wasn't for him letting us use his jet, I wouldn't have made the audition."

"True, but if you hadn't been up all night partying with Skee, you wouldn't have missed your flight in the first place." I caught Blair cutting her eyes at me and I was about to let her ass have it, but once again, Diamond stepped in, trying to be peacemaker.

"I think the three of us can agree that we all want Blair to be a huge superstar, but just wanting it isn't enough, we have to put in the work. Kennedy has been busting her ass to open doors for you, Blair."

"And I'm so appreciative of it. I tell Kennedy all the time how lucky I am to have her in my corner and you, too."

"That's true, but if you're serious about this you're going to have to decide what's more important to you:

pursuing your acting career or your relationship with Skee."

"So, you're saying I can't have both?"

"I'm saying it's going to be extremely difficult, especially when your boyfriend is already an established international superstar. He's used to things going his way and I'm sure compromising isn't a priority for him."

"I hear what you're saying, Diamond, but I don't think you all are giving Skee enough credit. He wants me to be a success and sometimes he can be a little overprotective, but that's because he knows how ruthless this business can be."

"Blair, for your sake, I hope Skee is one of your biggest supporters. I've seen how happy you are being with him. Actually, I've never seen you happier. All I'm saying is be careful and know what your priorities are."

"I do. My career comes first. I'll never waste precious time again. I learned that valuable lesson from dealing with Mike. I want to be a movie star and I'm willing to put in the necessary work to make it happen."

I heard the words leave Blair's mouth but it still wasn't making me a believer. Blair was full of determination but I could also tell that she lacked a lot of self-confidence. I wasn't sure if it all came from her dysfunctional relationship with Michael, childhood issues, or a combination of both. Whatever it was, if Blair didn't start recognizing the demons she was fighting and make a conscious decision to fight against them, I worried that Skee would have a much more negative influence on her than Michael ever did.

Blair

"Baby, I missed you," Skee said, before giving me a kiss.

"I missed you, too." It had only been a couple days since the last time we saw each other, but it seemed the more time we spent together; the more we hated being apart.

"Does that mean you'll be spending the night? I've gotten used to waking up next to you."

"I have to admit, I've gotten a little spoiled falling asleep in your arms.'"

"So, I guess that means you'll be staying the night."

"I'll think about it," I sighed, as if I really didn't want to.

"Oh, you'll think about it, huh," Skee said, before playfully tossing me down on the couch and then started tickling me.

"Stop!" I yelled, while giggling at the same time. But Skee wouldn't let up. He kept tickling me, until I was laughing so hard, the side of my stomach started to cramp. "That's enough!" I was finally able to get out between laughs.

"A'ight, you lil' crybaby," he chuckled and then

nuzzled the tip of his nose on the side of my neck.

"I always love when you do that," I mumbled, under my breath.

"I know you do," Skee replied, as his nuzzling turned into soft kisses sprinkling my neck. I arched my back and my hips began slightly shifting on the couch as I became more turned on by Skee's touch. He knew my neck was one of my major hot spots and every time he kissed me there, I instantly got wet and wanted to have sex. When his lips made their way to mine, we began exchanging passionate kisses, until the doorbell interrupted us.

"Please, don't stop," I pleaded, pulling Skee closer to me.

"I'm sure that's the delivery man. I have to get our food."

"Fine," I gasped, "but hurry back."

"I'll be back before you know it." While I waited for Skee to return, I stared up at the cathedral ceilings and started thinking about the conversation I had with Diamond and Kennedy the other day. Although I firmly believed that Skee was on my side and wanted me to reach my dreams, I couldn't shake what they said. It had been replaying in mind nonstop. I wanted to discuss my concerns with Skee, but it never seemed to be the right time.

"You ready to eat?" Skee said, coming back into the living room and snapping me out of my thoughts.

"Yes and that food smell delicious."

"I'm telling you this spot has the best Indian food in the city. Hold on one sec."

"Where are you going now?"

"To the kitchen. Nothing goes better with Indian Food then a nice bottle of red wine."

By the time Skee got back, my food was already on my plate and I had begun eating. "I know it might seem like I'm being greedy but I was starving," I said, taking another bite of vegetable rice.

"You know I love a woman who isn't afraid to eat," Skee smiled, handing me a glass of wine. By my second drink and a full stomach, I began feeling super relaxed. My slight buzz had me so comfortable, I thought now was the perfect time to have that conversation with Skee.

"Baby, do you want me to get the role I auditioned for?" I asked offhandedly, thinking a casual approach would work best.

"Of course, why would you ask me that?"

"I thought you did, but I just wanted to hear you say it."

"Are you sure that's all it is?"

"Yeah."

"So, that question has nothing to do with the conversation I had with Kennedy?"

"When did you and Kennedy have a conversation?" I questioned, pretending I had no idea what Skee was talking about. I didn't want him to know that both Diamond and Kennedy had voiced their concerns, so I figured it was best to play dumb.

"When we were in LA, I talked to Kennedy briefly when you had went to the spa. I told her I wanted you to go on tour with me. She said that wouldn't be able to happen if you got the part in the movie. So, I said I guess I hope you don't get it, but I didn't mean that seriously. Of course, I would prefer to have you on tour with me, but I know how important this is to you, so I want everything to work out."

"Thank you. I hope it works out, too, but I also wish I could go on tour with you. Unfortunately, I can't be two places at one time."

"When will you find out if you got the part?"

"I thought I would know by now but Kennedy believes we'll have an answer any day now."

"If, for some reason, you don't get the part, will you go on tour with me?"

"I don't want to think about not getting the part."

"I know but realistically you have to know that's a possibility."

"You're right but I guess I don't want to think about dealing with that sort of disappointment."

"I understand but, umm, traveling the world on a private jet, with first class accommodations, for a couple months isn't a bad alternative, is it?"

"When you put it like that, nope," I grinned. "I tell you what, although I'm extremely optimistic that I'll get the part, if I don't, then yes, I'll be more than happy to go on tour with you."

"That's an answer I can accept."

"Good, now get over here so we can finish what you started earlier," I said, reaching my hand out to Skee, pulling him down on the couch with me.

When I got to the heated rooftop bar, I spotted Kennedy

sitting down with a drink already in her hand. I was looking forward to getting a glass in my hand, too, but the elegant backdrop set against the incredible skyline of Manhattan always put me in a celebratory mood.

"Hey! You look beautiful, as always," Kennedy said, standing up to give me a hug when I walked up. "That dress looks amazing on you."

"Thanks! I actually got it when we went to LA. Skee picked it out. He said he thought the light gray and pink color combination made me look like a sexy angel. He's so silly," I laughed, thinking of him.

"It does look great on you."

"Here's your drink," The waitress said, handing me a champagne glass.

"Wow, you already ordered for me. Thanks!"

"I know what you like and I didn't want you to have to wait."

"OMG! You heard from Marcus and you want to celebrate. That's why you already ordered me champagne. Should we wait for Diamond? I'm sure she wants to be here to celebrate, too."

"Actually, Diamond couldn't make it."

"Damn! But that's okay, we can do this again. We never get tired of celebrating," I beamed.

"Blair, I did hear from Marcus," Kennedy said, putting her glass down, "but they decided to go with somebody else for the part."

"What!?" I felt my face turning red. "I really embarrassed myself going on and on about celebrating. We have absolutely nothing to celebrate," I said, gulping down my champagne. "Now, I see why you already ordered for me. It was a pity drink."

"Blair, you have nothing to feel bad about and do have a lot to celebrate. Six months ago, nobody knew who you were, now you're on all the blogs. Promoters want to pay you to host parties and you had an audition for a major film. That's amazing."

"You're right, it is. I just really had my heart set on getting this part."

"I know, beautiful, but there will be other roles," Kennedy said, gently stroking my hair. "I think it's important that you know it came down to you and one other actress. They loved you but the studio decided to go with the more established actress. So, please, don't think for one second you didn't do an incredible job. Trust me, that audition is going to lead to more opportunities for you."

"I hope you're right."

"I know I am. Have faith in me. Diamond and I are going to put everything into you. You will become a superstar. This is a minor bump. We'll regroup and figure it out."

"Okay, but I better get going."

"Already? But you haven't even had anything to eat."

"I lost my appetite."

"Are you headed back to the apartment? If so, we can share a cab."

"Skee's driver is actually downstairs waiting for me. He's at the studio. I'm meeting him after I leave here."

"Okay. Well, call me later if you want to talk. Blair, please stay optimistic."

"I will. I promise! As always, thanks for everything."

I gave Kennedy a hug and a wide smile before leaving; but when I reached downstairs, got inside the car, and was hidden behind the dark tinted windows, I broke down and cried. I felt like I had been punched in the chest. I had made the mistake of making myself believe this part was my destiny and it would be mine. Having to accept that I was wrong was ripping me up inside. I hated feeling this sort of pain and I wanted it to stop. I reached in my purse and got my cell phone.

"What's up, baby?"

"Do you still want me to go on that tour with you?"

"You know I do. That seat on the jet still has your name on it."

"Good, because I'll be on it."

Diamond

"Thanks for seeing me," I said to Renny, before I had even walked through the front door.

"You didn't leave me much choice," Renny scoffed, before stepping to the side, so I could come inside.

"I know we agreed not to see each other until my case was dismissed and shit cooled down, but this was too important."

"So, talk."

"Do you know a woman named Darcy Woods?"

"No, I don't," he said with a straight face.

"So, why are you the owner of her PR firm Woods Inc.?"

"If you're already aware that I know her, why ask the question?"

"Because I wanted to see if you would be honest with me. We've been doing business together long enough that I thought you would."

"Diamond, you know how I move. Being honest is never my first choice, but since you know the truth, my question now becomes: Why do you care?"

"Darcy has become a problem. I told you that I

was getting out of the drug business and I planned on partnering up with a very good friend of mine, to start our own PR firm. Darcy is spreading lies about my partner to sabotage her reputation, which will hurt our business. I want you to put a stop to it."

"First of all, I don't even get involved in the day to day operations of how Darcy runs that company. I'm simply the moneyman."

"I wouldn't come to you unless it was crucial. You have to stop Darcy because if not, this will become a lot bigger than a bitter ex-boss spreading lies about a former employee."

"A lot bigger like what?"

"I don't want to go into details, but I need you to trust me on this. Like you said, you're the moneyman. All you have to do is place one phone call, tell Darcy to back the fuck off from spreading lies about Kennedy, and to bow out of trying to get an account with a new movie studio."

"How am I supposed to explain this request to Darcy?"

"You and I both know you don't have to explain shit to Darcy. What you say goes, but I need you to make this happen ASAP."

"Say I clean this up for you, I'm going to need you to do something for me."

"What is it?"

"I haven't decided yet, but this is the second time you've come to me within the last few months, asking me to clean up some bullshit for you. I'm just putting you on notice that I will be collecting on what you owe and make sure you're ready to pay up when it's time."

"I'm prepared to do that."

"You sure? I can't miss that humongous rock on your finger. Are congratulations in order?"

"Yes," I said, looking down at my finger. "We're engaged."

"You've come a long way, Diamond. You went from dealing wit' that sorry ass nigga Rico to becoming engaged to a multi millionaire basketball player. You've done well for yourself. I understand you wanting to become completely legitimate, but once you make the decision to get in the game you'll never be completely out of it. It always finds a way to creep back up on you, at the most inconvenient times."

"I appreciate the warning, Renny, and you know how much respect I have for you. So, like I said, I'll pay up when you come to collect, just place that phone call to Darcy. Let me worry about everything else."

Renny nodded his head, letting me know he would take care of it and I made my exit. When I got in the car, I slammed my door and put my head down on the steering wheel for a moment. I was relieved I was able to get Renny to do what I asked, without revealing the reason behind it. I couldn't take the chance of telling him about the information Kennedy had on him and what she planned to do with it. If I had, I would be signing her death certificate, because no matter how much I pleaded and tried to convince Renny she would never use it, he would kill Kennedy, just to guarantee that she couldn't.

I also knew that Renny meant every word he said,

when he told me he would collect on what I owed him. I just prayed whatever he asked for I would be willing to deliver, because honestly, Renny wouldn't leave me a choice. But I couldn't worry about that right now. I had something much more important to deal with. This time next week, Rico would be dead.

"Baby, don't be so down. Next season, you all will win and get the ring," I said, trying to get Cameron out of his slump. Ever since they lost the East Coast Finals, Cameron had been moping around the house in a funk. I had been trying to figure out something we could do to get his mind off of it, but nothing seemed to work.

"We were so damn close. I'm sick of getting right there and then somebody fuckin' up, and there goes our season."

"I know, baby, but you have to keep your eyes on the prize. You guys are still a young team. I guarantee you next season this will be a different conversation. Until then, find something else to do, to get your mind off the game." I loved Cameron with all my heart but I was quickly finding out that being a basketball wife required you to be a resilient cheerleader, at all times.

"It's not that easy. I mean, do I need to start thinking about exercising my option?"

"I don't think so. You should never make an emotional decision; you'll regret it. Enjoy the offseason and think about your options when your mind is clear, and your emotions are out of it."

"You're right. Baby, I'm so lucky to have you,"

Cameron smiled, and then lifted me up in the air, before kissing me.

"I missed that smile. I'm so happy to see it again."

"It's all because of my future wife. It's true what they say. A great woman makes a man even better."

"You're so sweet. I love you."

"I love you too. I love you so much that I've come up with a great idea."

"Really...what?"

"You know how you said I need to find something to do to get my mind off the game?"

"Yes and you should. Why, did you come up with something already?"

"I did and you're the motivation."

"Me...what? I can't wait to hear this."

"Lets get married."

"Umm, once you put the ring on my finger and proposed, I already figured getting married was the next step."

"I mean lets get married now. Not at this very moment but in the next month or so."

"What! You can't be serious."

"Why can't we? What, are you not ready to marry me?"

"Of course I'm ready to marry you. I would marry you tomorrow."

"Then what's the problem?"

"We need to plan it. That takes time."

"That's what a wedding planner is for."

"I doubt they can put together a beautiful wedding in less than eight weeks."

"Trust me, when the money is right, you can make anything happen."

"So, baby you're serious about this. You really want to move forward?" My eyes widened and I felt a burst of exciting energy shoot through me.

"Hell yeah! Let's do it. Lets get married!"

I had allocated my entire day to killing Rico. I had been following him since this morning. I basically already knew how he moved from doing my own surveillance on him previously. I still wanted to be careful and not make any mistakes, so I was taking my time. But there was no doubt in my mind that today, Rico would die.

I watched as Rico entered into a side door to go inside a building. He seemed to frequent this same spot at least twice a week. I figured he was going there to either collect money or get product but that was irrelevant to me. I just like the location of the spot in the Bronx. The street was in the cut and didn't have a lot of foot traffic. I had also scanned the area and there weren't any cameras in the vicinity. I knew whatever business Rico was handling never took him longer than ten minutes, so I put my plan in motion.

I put the hoodie over my head and placed the dark sunglasses over my eyes. I then made a slight u-turn before backing up my rental car into the alley, right next to the entrance door Rico used. I grabbed my Glock and put on the silencer, while lying in wait until the precise moment I would make my move.

When I saw the door open, I stepped out of the

car with the gun in the front pocket of my hoodie. Rico didn't notice me and kept walking, until he heard my car door slam. I could tell he was startled because he jumped and with swiftness, he turned in the direction the noise came from. When Rico saw me he squinted his eyes, trying see if he recognized who I was. With the hoodie and sunglasses it was almost impossible.

I wanted Rico to know exactly who was about to take him out of this world, so I lowered my sunglasses and our eyes locked. Rico began slowly walking towards me, as if to make sure he was seeing shit correctly. I remained in my position, forcing him to come closer. I wanted Rico as far into the alley and away from the street, as possible.

"Diamond, is that you?" he asked, as if he was unsure and his mind was playing tricks on him. When he stepped a few feet closer, I simply smiled. "What the fuck is you doing here?" Rico barked, now only a few feet away from me.

"I thought we needed to talk."

"Talk about what and why the fuck is you in the motherfuckin' alley with a hoodie and sunglasses on. You hidin' from somebody?" he said, in a joking way.

"I was but there's no need to hide now."

"What you want? Is something wrong wit' Destiny?"

"Nope. I came here to ask you a question."

"That's what a phone is for."

"I needed to ask you this in person," I said, continuing to grip my gun. Rico was so busy trying to be slick with the tongue that he wasn't even aware that

I had a gun in my front hoodie pocket.

"Then ask the fuckin' question, so I can get outta here," he scoffed, as he now was standing directly in front of me.

"Parish told me you were the one that set me up to be robbed. As much as I detest you, I would never do no bullshit like that to you. Why? One reason, you're Destiny's father. I'm our daughter's mother, but clearly you place no value in that."

"Bitch, please. I don't give a fuck about you being Destiny's mother. Yo' ass can be replaced."

"So, you're not denying you were the one responsible for Parish breaking into my home, putting a gun to my head, and stealing money from me that goes towards taking care of our daughter?"

"Nah, I ain't denying shit. It was me and I would do that shit again. Just 'cause you done had a minor come up don't get brand new. You still the same bum bitch you were when I dropped that seed in you."

At that moment, I realized shooting Rico would be too easy. I wanted to get into the rental car and run over his body over and over again. In my mind that's what he deserved...to be tortured. Unfortunately, I didn't have time for all that.

"You truly are a bitch ass nigga. You ain't got no heart and I wish on everything that you weren't Destiny's father."

"Too late, I am. For the rest of your pathetic life I'm gonna remind you of that shit, too, so deal wit it."

"I don't have to deal wit' shit. You underestimated me, Rico. I could handle us disliking each other, but you crossed the line and what you did is unacceptable."

"Ho, whatever. What the fuck you gon' do, tell yo' man? I want you to do that shit, so I can tell him all the foul shit you done."

"Luckily for me, you'll never have that chance." I pulled out the Glock with such speed the bullets started flying in Rico's direction, before he could even blink. "How does it feel looking into the eyes of the woman who is going to take you out of this world?"

Rico stood there, stunned. Once shit clicked and what was going down registered in his head, Rico tried to take off running, but I had already unloaded half of my clip and most of the bullets had hit my target. I continued firing, until my clip was empty and Rico lay bloodied, and motionless. I jumped back into the car and drove off, without looking back.

Kennedy

"This place is incredible!" I said, putting my hands up in the air with excitement.

"I knew you would think so. When the real estate agent showed me this space, I knew it would be perfect for our company."

"Who wouldn't love it...an incredible, open space with a loft and the location in Midtown. This is some Baller Bitch shit foreal!" I said, slapping Diamond's hand.

"I want the industry to know that we're serious and about our business when we make our introduction."

"I can't believe how great this week is turning out for me. First, Marcus calls and says that Darcy not only admitted to his partner that she lied on me, but she was also pulling out of wanting the account, so now it's ours and then you surprise me with this amazing space for our company. This day, this week, this month can't get any better. Diamond, I'm so glad I listened to you and waited before moving forward with my plan. It all worked out."

"Sometimes, all it takes is a little faith."

"I still can't help but wonder what made Darcy

come clean."

"Who knows, but there's no need to put any more energy into Darcy Woods. We have much bigger things to focus on."

"You're right...hold on a minute, that's Marcus calling now. He probably wants to know if I had a chance to look over the agreement he sent over. Hey Marcus!"

"Hey Kennedy, so glad you answered."

"Of course, we're about to be doing some major business together, so I always answer for my clients."

"That's good to know, but this is regarding something else."

"What is it?"

"Is Blair still interested in that role?"

"Excuse me!"

"The other actress got the lead in another movie and backed out. The part is Blair's if she wants it."

"I can't believe I'm hearing this. Of course she still wants the role."

"I was hoping you'd say that. We would need her on the first flight tomorrow morning."

"She'll be on it."

"Great, I'll get the ticket information over to you."

"Make that three tickets. I'll be coming and so will my partner, Diamond."

"No problem. I'll get the hotel accommodations over to you, also. She'll probably be filming for about six weeks; it might be shorter, but that's the timeline we're going with."

"Got it. We'll see you tomorrow and thanks, Marcus." After I ended the call I went crazy. "OMG! OMG!

Blair got the movie role!"

"Shut the fuck up! Are you serious? YESSSSSS!" Diamond and I held each other and jumped around, doing the happy dance.

"I was just saying this day, this week, this month couldn't get any better and this happens. Wow! We're headed to Hollywood, baby!"

"As much as I would love to go, I can't."

"Why?"

"Remember, I told you we're having the wedding in like eight weeks."

"That's right! How can I forget? I'm sorry."

"No worries. You go to LA, and hold it down with Blair. I'll be here in New York, getting my wedding together and our office space. Of course, both of you better be here for the wedding, because you all are the bridesmaids."

"We'll be done filming by then but regardless, we will be there representing."

"Now, go and tell Blair the great news. I would go with you, but Cameron and I are meeting with the wedding planner in thirty minutes."

"I totally understand. Go plan your wonderful wedding and I'm going to go tell Blair the exciting news!"

"I know you all have to leave early in the morning, but let's try got get together tonight and have a celebratory toast."

"Will do," I said, giving Diamond a kiss on the cheek, before heading out.

"Kennedy, hi! What was so urgent that you had to see me in person, instead of just telling me on the phone," Blair said when she opened the door.

"Is Skee here?" I asked, cautiously.

"Yeah, we're actually packing."

"Where are you all going?"

"Remember, I told you since I didn't get the movie role I was going on tour with him."

"I didn't realize that was so soon."

"Yes, I'm actually excited. Traveling the world on a private jet...not too shabby."

"Babe, who was at the door?" Skee yelled out.

"It's Kennedy."

"Oh, she wanted to come over and tell you goodbye before you leave," Skee said, as he came down the stairs.

"No, I actually had to tell her something a little more important...make that a lot more important. Marcus just called me a little while ago and the part is yours."

"What! You're lying! Don't play with me like that, Kennedy!"

"I'm not playing. The other actress got the lead in another movie and backed out of the film, so they want you. I call it divine intervention."

"I call it my destiny," Blair beamed.

"She can't take the role," Skee stated, walking up on us. Blair and I both turned towards him with utter shock on our faces.

"Baby, what are talking about? You know how much I want this role."

"You didn't get the role, remember. You weren't

their first choice. They gave it to another actress and now they're offering it to you because she can't do it. Fuck them! You don't need the role."

"I don't care if I wasn't their first choice. I have an opportunity to prove that I should've been and I'm taking it."

"We're supposed to be leaving tomorrow."

"I can still come if only for a couple weeks, until it's time to start filming."

"Actually you have to be on a flight first thing in the morning. They want you to start filming immediately. You'll be there for six weeks."

"Fuck that! You're not going!" Skee barked, tossing down a carryon bag he was holding. "You want to change our plans for some bullshit role!"

"This isn't bullshit to me. I want to make something of myself. I want to be somebody."

"You are somebody...you're my fuckin' woman," he yelled. "What else do you need?"

Blair stood there with her arms folded and head down. I could see how torn she was. It was evident to me that Skee had a much stronger hold on Blair than she even realized.

"Blair, what are you going to do?" I finally asked, putting an end to the eerie silence.

"Didn't you hear what I said? Blair won't be taking the part, so that means she won't be coming." I ignored Skee and didn't even acknowledge what he said. Instead, I made eye contact with Blair waiting for her response.

"I'll call you, Kennedy."

"Huh? What are you saying to me right now?"

"I'm saying that I need to speak to Skee alone and I'll call you later." I wanted to go over to Blair and shake the shit out of her, but I kept my composure. I knew that wasn't the right move to make. I couldn't force Blair to get on that flight tomorrow to LA, it had to be her decision.

"Ok, I'll be waiting for your call."

When I left, before the door had even closed all the way, I heard Skee starting right back up with the yelling. The dude had serious control issues and I had a bad feeling he was going to convince Blair to turn down the role and go with him. As my heart began to sink, I noticed Diamond calling me.

"Hey."

"Why you sound like somebody died? I was expecting to hear you and Blair celebrating."

"The way things seem right now, I won't be celebrating shit," I sighed.

"What happened?"

"You mean who happened. "

"What you mean "who"? I'm not following you."

"Skee."

"Oh gosh, what has he done now?"

"Blair was at his house, so I went over there to give her the news. They were packing because they're supposed to be leaving tomorrow, to start his tour. If Skee has his way, which it's looking like he might, they still will be."

"You're telling me that Blair is turning down the role to go on tour with Skee?"

"I'm saying it's a strong possibility. As usual, when

things don't go his way, Skee started having one of his temper tantrums, but I'm telling you Diamond, I saw the look in Blair's eyes, she's fallen hard for him."

"I'm about to call Blair right now. This isn't the time to be dick dumb. She has to get on that plane tomorrow. This role is going to change her life."

"I know that and you know that, but if it isn't what Blair wants more than anything, then it doesn't matter. It has to be her decision and hers alone."

"I can't believe Blair's this close and about to throw it all away for Skee."

"I know," I huffed, wishing I could snap my finger and zap Skee out of Blair's life.

"So, when will you know what her decision is?"

"She said she needed to speak to Skee alone and would call me."

"This some bullshit. You sure I shouldn't call her?"

"I'm positive. I want Blair on that plane just as much as you do, but if she chooses Skee over her career, then so be it. We'll have to deal with it."

"I hear you. Keep me posted. I want to know what happens."

"Will do."

When I got off the phone with Diamond, I hopped in the cab and headed home. The drive seemed like the longest ride of my life. I was trying to will my phone to ring and have it be Blair, telling me she was coming, but no such call came. I knew this was going to be a long night. I doubted I would get any sleep because I would be keeping one eye on my cell, praying for that call from Blair.

When I got inside my apartment, I tossed the keys down, took a shower, and continued my night of waiting. I was tempted to pull out my suitcase and start packing for LA, but my gut told me it would be a waste of time, because we wouldn't be going. I eventually fell asleep on the couch, accepting that.

When I started waking up from my sleep, I thought my mind was playing tricks on me. It felt like I was stuck between reality and a dream, but I couldn't figure out which was which.

"You better get up if you want us to catch that flight. If we miss it this time, we don't have a private jet waiting on us."

"Blair," I mumbled with my eyes halfway open.

"That's right. Get up sleepy girl."

"I can't believe you're here. I thought..."

"I know what you thought," Blair said, cutting me off. "I told you I wanted this more than anything and I meant it."

"What about Skee?"

"He's not happy but I told him after I kicked ass on this movie, I would join him on tour. It'll all work out."

"You made the right decision. You won't regret it."

"I know. It was the only decision I could make. As you can see," Blair said, pointing to her two large suitcases, "I'm already packed. So, you better get up and get ready. Here, I even stopped and got you some Starbucks to assist you with that."

"Nothing like some caffeine to get me going. Hollywood, here we come!"

Blair

"It's a wrap! Can you believe it?!" Kennedy exclaimed, jumping up and down. "I remember when I said that to you, after you did your first music video."

"Yeah, the one where I met Skee," I smiled, thinking back to when we first met.

"Now, you're wrapping your first major movie. How amazing it that? Baby girl, I'm so proud of you I don't know what to do! Give me a hug!"

"I love you, Kennedy, I really do."

"I love you, too."

Kennedy and I hugged each other so tightly. It seemed like only yesterday we arrived in LA to start shooting and now I was done. It had been this non-stop rollercoaster ride of living out my dream, but I was happy it was over, at least for now. I missed Skee way more than I thought I would and I couldn't wait to be with him again. Although we talked frequently, it wasn't the same as being right by his side.

"So, does that mean you don't mind if I go join Skee for the last couple weeks of his tour?"

"Of course, you deserve it. Go have some fun with

your man."

"Great, then I'll make it back in time for Diamond and Cameron's wedding. I can't believe they were able to plan it so quickly."

"You know when Diamond puts her mind to something, she can make anything happen and long money also helps."

"Of course," we both laughed. "Let me call Skee. He swore the shooting was going to go overschedule and I wouldn't make it in time to join him. Wait till he hears the good news. Hold on a sec, somebody just sent me a text to a link. What the fuck!" I screamed, then fell down on the chair and put my head down.

"Blair, what's wrong?"

I couldn't say a word and just handed my iPhone to Kennedy.

"That sonofabitch!"

"How could he? I'm over here working, trying to make something of myself, while Skee is on a yacht with a bikini clad woman kissing him on his chest and I'm positive those kisses led to fucking and sucking. How can he do this to me? I don't understand," I cried out, shaking my head.

"Because he's a self-centered asshole, that's why. He doesn't deserve you, Blair. Skee wants a woman who is willing to build their entire life around him. He's showing you if you don't do what he wants, then he'll find somebody that will. Do you really want to give your heart to a man like that? Speaking of the devil, here is Skee calling you now," Kennedy said, handing me my phone.

"What do you want?"

"Blair, I know you've seen the pics but it's not what you think."

"Really? That's not your chest that woman has her tongue all over...exactly."

"You know I wanted you here with me."

"Yeah and right before I saw that pic, I was about to call and let you know I was done filming. I was coming to be with you for the rest of your tour."

"You can still come."

"You must be crazy if you think I'm coming anywhere near you. I'm done!" I yelled, as the tears kept pouring out.

"Yo, calm down. You don't mean that. I made a mistake. I needed you to be with me and you weren't, so I slipped."

"So, you fuckin' somebody else is *my* fault? You're unbelievable. You know what, go fuck yourself. Like I said, I'm done!" I ended the call and tossed the phone down on the chair. Skee kept calling back, but I refused to answer.

"Blair, I know this is hard for you, but you're doing the right thing. Your career is going to take off and the last thing you need is to be stressed by some spoiled, self-centered rapper."

"Everything you're saying is exactly right. You know, I think I was really starting to fall in love with him. I wasn't ready to admit it but..." I paused as I tried to get my composure. "I did fall in love and look what he did," I said, between sniffles.

"It's going to be okay. I promise you," Kennedy

said, rubbing my back. "Fuck Skee Patron. Within a year, you'll be a bigger star than him and he'll regret ever shitting on you."

♥

Diamond's wedding day had approached so fast. I still couldn't believe today Diamond would be a married woman. One day she was sharing her engagement news, the next she had set a date and planned a lavish ceremony. In true Diamond form, with a limited amount of time she hired the perfect wedding planner to make everything go off effortlessly.

When I got back to New York, I was actually relived Diamond had so much going on between wedding preparations, and her and Kennedy getting their office together for the grand opening. Being busy kept me from going back to Skee. Between all his gifts, the flowers, and non-stop phone calls, I was tempted to go back to him several times, but having Kennedy and Diamond in my corner kept me strong.

"Diamond, you have to be the most beautiful bride I've ever seen." And she was. Diamond had on a stunning, off-the-shoulder gown of French Alencon lace and rosettes, complete with a 12-foot train. "I think I'm going to cry," I said, staring at someone who was more than just my best friend, but was like a sister to me.

"Blair, don't cry," she said wiping the tears from my eyes. "You're going to mess up your makeup." We both gave a half laugh, trying to stop not only my tears, but also Diamond's.

"Both of you stop, right now!" Kennedy demanded.

"Blair is right, you look beyond amazing. I still can't believe you're getting married, but if anyone deserves happiness, it's you." Kennedy gave Diamond a hug, which turned into a group hug.

"I want both of you to know that just because I'm getting married doesn't mean I'm not part of the gang anymore. We're still going to have our weekly get together for lunch or dinner, and our monthly spa dates."

"You best believe it's not going to stop. If Blair and I have to come to your place and drag you out, we will. Our sisterly bond is going to last forever," Kennedy declared; now tearing up herself, as we held each other's hands.

"Diamond, it's time." We all turned towards the door and saw Diamond's Uncle, who was walking her down the aisle, standing there.

"Wow, in a few short minutes you'll be exchanging vows and then you will be Mrs. Diamond Robinson. Are you ready?" I asked, enthusiastically.

"I'm more than ready. I dreamed about this day my entire life, but never did I believe I would receive such an amazing man to be my husband. Ladies, I'm proof that dreams do come true."

"Yes, you are." Kennedy and I air kissed Diamond goodbye and took our positions as the bridesmaids.

"Make sure Destiny doesn't trip as she throws the rose petals down the aisle," Diamond yelled out, as we were walking out the door.

"We won't," we all laughed. When we walked in the hallway, there was Destiny waiting anxiously, holding her grandmother's hand. In her other hand she had a white basket full of rose petals. She looked absolutely adorable in her pink ruffled dress.

"Destiny looks so happy. I'm glad she doesn't know about her dad," Kennedy stated, as we stood and watched the little girl from a distance.

"I know but what if he doesn't pull through? Diamond has been through enough and as much as she doesn't like Rico, to have to tell Destiny that her dad is dead would be devastating for her." A deep sadness came over me, thinking about how badly this would affect Destiny.

"That's why I'm hoping he makes it. Destiny adores her dad."

"But it doesn't look good. He has been in a coma for weeks. Diamond even mentioned that the doctor doesn't even think he's going to come out of his coma, but Rico's mother refuses to give up hope and take him off life support. She believes in her heart that her son will wake up."

"For Destiny's sake, I hope she's right."

"We'll have to finish this conversation later. The music has started. It's showtime," I said, grabbing Kennedy's hand so we could walk down the aisle.

Being at the wedding, surrounded by such beauty, happiness, and love, I couldn't help but think about Skee. My heart ached for him but the pain he caused by cheating on me hurt a lot worse. By the time I realized Diamond was walking down the aisle, I had got back together, broke up, and got back together with Skee over a hundred times in my head. *Blair, STOP thinking about Skee. This is Diamond's wedding day. Get him out of your head, at least for the duration of the ceremony,* I screamed to myself.

I noticed Kennedy looking over at me, as if she knew my mind was someplace else. I got myself together and focused on Diamond, who was truly a vision as she walked down the aisle. Cameron stared at Diamond with nothing but adoration in his eyes.

As they exchanged vows, their undying love for each other was obvious to everyone in attendance. It was too beautiful for words to even describe. I don't think there was a dry eye in the building. Then, as if watching a scene from any bride's worst wedding ceremony moment, some woman seemed to appear out of nowhere, interrupting Cameron and Diamond, as they were exchanging their vows.

"Does Cameron have a baby mother or an ex-girlfriend we didn't know about?" Kennedy snapped.

"If he does, Diamond never mentioned it to me."

"Then who the hell is this woman?"

I glanced over in Diamond's direction and her facial expression was full of confusion, just like ours.

"Do you know that woman?" I heard Diamond ask Cameron.

"Hell no and where is security?" After I heard Cameron exchange those words with Diamond, he then turned to one of his best men and whispered something.

"Somebody get security and have this woman escorted out of here." Diamond demanded, clearly annoyed and rightly so. Some men who were wedding guests stood up and grabbed the woman from both sides.

"Let go of me," she screamed. "I'm not going anywhere, until you hear what I have to say," she continued, breaking free from the men. The entire venue went silent waiting to hear what the woman had to say. "I'm Rico's girlfriend. He came out of his coma today and told me everything. It was you! You were the one who tried to murder Destiny's father and you're going to pay for it!"

All you heard were loud gasps erupt. Everybody was looking at each other as if seeking confirmation that what they heard the woman say was correct. Then they started eyeing Diamond, waiting for her to say something, but she seemed to be in shock.

"Diamond, do you know this woman? What is she talking about?" Cameron questioned. But Diamond stood there speechless. The silence had everyone on edge.

We all seemed to lean forward simultaneously, as if it would force Diamond to open her mouth and talk. She turned and glanced in our direction and then back at Cameron, before finally speaking. "I can explain."

Diamond

All eyes were on me, as everyone waited to hear what I would say next. The intense stares had me beyond uncomfortable, but the uncertainty on Cameron's face had me feeling the most fucked up. How would I explain this shit to him? I knew I had a limited amount of time to speak up and that window of opportunity was closing quickly. When I felt my knees about to buckle, I said "fuck it" to myself and began letting the lies take on a life of their own.

"None of this is true. How dare you come in here and interrupt our wedding! This is supposed to be one of the happiest days of my life and you're trying to ruin it with your vicious lies! If Rico did say those things to you, then clearly he is just a man scorned and he's using you to spread his lies." I waited for a moment, to try and get a read on whether or not I came across as believable. When Blair and Kennedy walked over and gently rubbed my shoulders, I thought that was a good sign.

"Get her out of here...now!" Cameron barked, before nodding towards his men to have the woman removed.

"I'm telling the truth! It was her!" the woman screamed out, as she was practically dragged out of the venue.

"Let's take a break. I'm sure you need a moment to get yourself together after what just happened," Cameron suggested.

"No...no...no," I said, shaking my head. "I want to continue, right now."

"Are you sure?" I could see the genuine concern in Cameron's face.

"I'm positive. I want to move forward. I refuse to let Rico and his lies destroy our day. This is our moment and we will have it—not later, but right now."

Cameron gave me the most loving smile. "Then, so be it, let's do this."

I felt like such a fraud, deceiving Cameron into believing I was some sweet, innocent woman he fell in love with. But I wanted this moment of happiness in my life—scratch that—I *needed* it desperately and I wasn't going to let sorry-ass Rico take it away from me. We would take our vows before God, our family, and friends, and I would spend the rest of my life being the best wife possible to Cameron.

After the reception, Cameron and I immediately got on a private plane and headed to our honeymoon destination. I had no idea where that would be, but it didn't matter. I was now Mrs. Cameron Robinson and it was the best feeling in the world. I wanted to bottle these emotions and carry them around with me forever.

"We're in Turks and Caicos," I beamed, when we arrived at the resort center.

"Yep. I remember you said you always wanted to come here for a vacation. So, I thought it would be perfect for our honeymoon."

"Perfect is an understatement. And we're at Parrot Cay, one of the most private resorts."

"It gets even better."

"How does it get better than this?"

"You'll see." Before I could ask Cameron another question, a man was escorting us to a buggy. I decided not to ask any questions and wait to see where we ended up. After a five-minute ride, we arrived to our destination.

"Where are we?" I finally had to ask.

"This is the Sanctuary Villa. It's the resort's most secluded part. It's just you and me, baby. Besides a couple of butlers and a personal chef at our beck and call."

"Get the hell outta here! I can't believe you did this for me. Damn, I love you!" I screamed, jumping into Cameron's arms.

"I love you too, Mrs. Robinson."

This place certainly didn't disappoint. It was a honeymoon paradise. It was more beautiful than anything I could've ever imagined. There were acres of lush gardens, tropic flora, and gorgeous beaches. There were candles all around the suite to enhance the place's romance. From the second floor you had a perfect view of the island, as well as access to a private beach and infinity pool.

"Baby, I know this might sound a little tacky, but I have to ask, how much does staying at a place like this cost? I mean, I've never seen anything like this."

"Twenty-thousand a night, but nothing is too much for my wife and the love of my life," Cameron said, wrapping his strong muscular arms around me and placing his soft lips against mine. All I could think was my mother and grandmother must've been praying extra hard for me, to have been blessed with such a wonderful man to be my husband.

Kennedy

"I have an interview set up for you tomorrow and they want to do the photo shoot that will accompany the article on Friday."

"I'll pass."

"Excuse me? What do you mean you'll pass?" I asked, frowning at Blair.

"The last five interviews I've done, all they want to discuss is my now non-existent relationship with Skee. I'm sick of that shit," Blair complained.

"I can understand that being somewhat nerve-racking, but that movie you shot hasn't been released yet, and you don't have anything else going on right now. If talking about Skee keeps you in the media, then so be it. It's better for people to see your face than for you to just disappear and they forget about you."

"I don't know, Kennedy. This isn't working for me. I feel like I'm using his name to stay relevant and we're not even together anymore. I want people to be interested in me, not who my ex-boyfriend is."

"Blair, when you decided to step into the world of entertainment, you have to be willing to play the game.

Even when you are the star of major movies and you become the next Tyler Blake or Halle Berry, people are going to be interested in your private life. But the bigger your name becomes, based on what you're doing and accomplishing, the less you'll have to discuss things like that. You haven't gotten to that point yet in your career, but there is no doubt in my mind that you will. Until then, you have to deal with the downside."

"That's the thing, I don't know if I can." Blair had this sadness in her eyes and I had the feeling this had much more to do with having to discuss her private life.

"Blair, is there something else going on with you?"

"Having to talk about Skee all the time, in these interviews, is making it harder for me to get over him. It's like I have to relive the bad times, which then makes me think about the good times."

"Now I get it. You want to get back with Skee," I stated, as my eyes pierced directly into Blair's.

"I know, you must think I'm such a loser," Blair said, putting her head down as if she felt ashamed.

"I don't think you're a loser. I just think you're a woman who believes she's in love," I reasoned, tapping my pen down against the notepad on top of my desk.

"I really do think he's sorry for cheating on me."

"I've seen all the gifts and flowers being delivered to the apartment. That doesn't make a man sorry for cheating. It means he can afford to try and buy you back."

"So, that's what you think, Skee is trying to buy me back?"

"I think that Skee is a narcissistic, immature prick, who likes for everything to go his way. You may not believe this, but he wanted you to see him on the yacht with that other woman."

"What do you mean by that?"

"He's playing mind games with you. Because you decided to take that movie, he felt you chose your career over him. He was sending you a message, that if you don't put him first, then he will replace you. Do you want to give your heart to a man that cruel?"

"Kennedy, I know you mean well, but I think you're wrong about your assessment of Skee."

"No, I'm not. When those pictures came out he expected you to be upset, but he also thought it would make you come running back to him. You know, to secure your position in his life. When he realized it didn't work and you were cutting him off, that's why he has been sending you gifts non-stop. It's not because Skee is sorry, he just doesn't want to lose his "new" prized possession, which currently happens to be you."

"So, you don't think that maybe he just made a mistake and wants another chance to make it right?"

"Nope. But it doesn't matter what I think, it's what you believe."

Blair stood up from her chair and began pacing the floor. I hated to see her so torn. As much as I detested Skee, the spark in Blair's eyes seemed to be fading without him. I couldn't grasp why he had such a hold over her, but he did. But I believed if Blair could just be strong and not give into her urge to go back to him, that with time she could shake her unhealthy addiction to Skee.

"Blair, listen. Give yourself a few days to think

things over, before making any sort of decision about Skee. Go on this interview and do the photo shoot. After you get that done, and you still want to reach out to Skee, then do so."

"Really?" Blair turned around and gave me a confused stare.

"Yes. I want you to be happy, but I honestly think if you give yourself a little time, you'll realize you can be happy without Skee. So, what do you say?"

"You're always such the voice of reason. I think that's a great idea."

"I'm glad you do. So, I'll confirm the interview for tomorrow and text you all the info for the photo shoot Friday."

"Sounds good. Well, let me get out of here. I have a hair appointment that I don't want to miss," Blair said, grabbing her purse. "I'll talk to you later."

"Bye," I smiled with a quick wave. Once I saw Blair get on the elevator, I got on the phone. "Hey girl, I need you to do me a huge favor. If you can make this happen, I owe you."

Blair

I woke up and the first thing I did was reach over to grab my iPhone. In the last few weeks it had become a habit, since Skee would always greet me with a "Miss You" text in the morning. I hated myself for missing him so much. But I hated myself even more when I looked at my messages and there was none from Skee. I felt this nauseating feeling in the pit of my stomach.

Why didn't Skee send me a text this morning? Does he no longer miss me? Maybe he's finally decided to give up on me and move on. I'm not ready to let him go, I thought to myself. I went to my favorites and scrolled to his name. I was about to press call, but quickly placed my phone down.

"Blair, you have to be strong. Think about what Kennedy said. Give yourself a few more days and don't make any decisions until then," I said out loud, trying to talk myself out of giving into my desire to call Skee. Between battling myself, I realized what time it was and that I needed to take a shower and get to the photo shoot. Surprisingly, I was actually looking forward to it, if only to get my mind off Skee for a few hours.

When I arrived to the huge studio loft in Soho, the spot was already jumpin'. J Cole was blaring from the speakers; it was the stylist, makeup artist, and just random people everywhere. This definitely wasn't a closed set. But hey, I was no Rihanna, so I wasn't in the position to ask for one. Right when I was about to ask someone where I needed to go, a super bubbly Asian chick greeted me.

"Hi, you must be Blair. I recognized you for always being on the blogs with Skee Patron. That video you did with him is still one of my favorites."

"Thanks," I grinned, thinking to myself *here we go again.*

"So, I'm going to get you over to hair and makeup. Would you like something to drink?"

"Sure, a Red Bull would be great. I need a boost."

"No problem. I'll get that for you. If you need anything let me know. I'm Natalie, and I'll be your go-to girl for the day."

"Cool."

"Oops! Quick detour," Natalie giggled, stopping mid walk. "Let's go over to wardrobe first. I want to see what items are going to work for you, because that might inspire the hair and makeup people."

"Sure. I always love looking at the clothes, anyway."

"Well, there are no clothes."

"Huh? I don't understand."

"Oh, you're not going to be naked or anything. But

this is for our swimsuit issue. So, you'll be wearing some super cool bikinis and a monokini."

"You're kidding me right?"

"I'm serious. Your publicist or agent or whoever didn't tell you?"

"Nope."

"It that a problem? I mean, you look like you have a great body."

"No, that's fine. But skip the Red Bull. I don't need anything that might give my stomach a slight bulge."

"I totally understand," Natalie beamed, playfully tapping my arm. If only some of her chirpiness could rub off on me, then maybe this whole bathing suit thing would be more tolerable.

Natalie, the stylist, and I went through a ton of bathing suit choices, until we picked a few different options. Then, they were matched up with some ridiculously gorgeous heels.

"These are all really hot," I commented, as we made our way to the makeup chair.

"Yeah, and you're going to look amazing in them, especially when they have the fans blowing, your skin glistening, and the hot guy. These pictures are going to be beyond beautiful," Natalie smiled, being the ultimate cheerleader.

"So, there is going to be a guy in the pictures with me?"

"Oh, yeah! Girl, this might be front magazine cover material."

"Who's the guy?" I asked, curious to know who it was.

"It's.... oh, I'm going to let it be a surprise," Natalie quipped, quickly changing her mind about revealing who it was. "All I'll say is he is super sexy and the ladies and some men, I'm sure, are going to love to see him with his shirt off."

"Okay," I said, thinking that could be a bunch of different men, so I would have to wait and see. One thing I was happy about was that I had my own dressing room to get hair and makeup done. Plus, change into those itty-bitty bathing suits. I thought I had a pretty decent body, but I wasn't really secure about flaunting it in front of strangers, with lights and cameras on me. But this was the life I chose, so I had to make the most of it. I sat back and let the glam squad do their thing. I never liked to look at myself until they were completely done. I always loved seeing the before and after results. The transformation would give me this weird type of high.

I lost track of time as I flipped through magazines, bopped my head to the music, and before long the glam squad was done. When I walked over to the mirror and looked at myself, I was unbelievably pleased.

"Amazing. I think this is the best hair and makeup job anybody has done on me."

"Thank you," both ladies said simultaneously. I wasn't just saying that either. They had me looking like some sort of seductive, modern mermaid. I actually felt beautiful, something I hadn't been feeling in a very long time.

"We'll leave out, so you can put on the bikini. But call us if you need us."

"Will do and thanks again, ladies. You both really

did an incredible job. I wasn't expecting this."

Even in my moment of feeling beautiful, Skee hadn't escaped my mind. I reached in my purse for my phone, hoping I would see a missed call or a text from him, but there was nothing.

"They're ready for you," I heard Natalie say, after knocking on the door. I glanced at myself one last time in the mirror and felt tears developing in my eyes. I started coughing, because I remember hearing that if you wanted to fight back tears, coughing was one of the ways you could do it. It seemed to be working, so I forced a smile before stepping out my dressing room.

"I'm ready!" I beamed, as Natalie, the hair stylist, and makeup artist all stared at me.

"Wow!" they echoed in unison.

"That aqua and gold sequined bikini with those sky high Jimmy Choo's is everything," Natalie commented as she twirled me around. "Add a little more shimmer to her body," she told the makeup artist, as she did a full head to toe inspection. Natalie was extra bubbly, but I could tell she clearly was about her business. She was paying extra close attention to every detail.

After they were finished dolling me up, Natalie led me to the front, where the photographer, a camera crew, and tons of lights awaited me.

"I didn't know this was being filmed."

"Yeah, we're doing a behind the scenes to show online. You know, to build up the anticipation of the magazine release."

"Whatever works," I replied, being taken aback by the perfectly built man standing in front of the camera.

His back was to me so I couldn't see his face but from the angle I was seeing, he didn't have a drop a fat on his chiseled body. Dare I say, seeing all that chocolate flesh and muscles had me catching my breath.

"Isn't he amazing looking," Natalie commented, clearly reading the expression on my face. "Wait to you see him from the front. It only gets better."

Then, in a matter of seconds, all my delight went straight to shambles when the picture perfect creation turned around and our eyes met. I could tell by the disdain in his eyes he wasn't pleased to see me, either.

"Kirk, this is Blair, Blair this is Kirk," Natalie said, introducing us, as if she was proud of herself. I extended my hand, trying to keep things professional. "The two of you are going to have women and men all over the world lusting after you, when they see these pictures," Natalie continued, until Kirk interrupted her.

"I know Blair," Kirk said, in an ultra dry tone, refusing to shake my hand.

"Listen, Kirk, if you have a problem doing the photo shoot with me, then they can get somebody else."

"Wait, what are you talking about, Blair? You're standing there looking like the ultimate glam girl, why would we want to use somebody else?"

"Umm, it's pretty obvious that Kirk would rather not do this shoot with me." Natalie turned towards Kirk and he didn't say a word, letting his silence speak for him.

"I'm sure Kirk is fine with doing the photo shoot with you," Natalie smiled, determined to make the situation work.

"Look, I would prefer if you could get another model here...you know, if it's not too late."

"As a matter of fact, it is too late," Natalie shot back, in a stern tone that I didn't even think she was capable of using. "We're all professionals here. So, we're going to get this photo shoot done and make it front cover worthy. Are we clear?" She gave both Kirk and I hard stares.

"Got it," I replied.

"Me too," Kirk, added, with annoyance in his voice, before walking off.

"Hold on a sec," Natalie said, pulling me to the side. "Blair, I don't know what happened between you and Kirk, but I need you to leave it off this set. This is a huge issue for us and we need it to be flawless. You follow me?"

"I totally understand, but honestly I think you should be having this conversation with Kirk, because I'm going to do my job."

"No, I'm having the conversation with the right person. With the way you look in that bikini, you should be able to get Kirk over any hostility he has towards you, at least long enough to get him through this photo shoot."

"I'll do my best," I promised, ready to get this over with, before it had even started. Natalie was asking me to pull off a miracle. If she knew Kirk like I did, she would know that if you rub him the wrong way, he had no problem holding a grudge.

"Okay, Kirk, you stand over there with both hands on the basketball. Blair, you lean behind him putting your right arm over his chest and then look off to the side," the photographer directed.

I did what the photographer asked and Kirk jerked his body forward, as if it repulsed him to feel my touch. I glanced over at Natalie and could see her face cringing up. I realized Kirk was not going to make this easy for me and I didn't know how to handle this, besides running off the set, getting my shit, and exiting the building. But I knew that would be the wrong move.

No matter how much notoriety I had been getting from dating Skee, being on the blogs daily, and in a few magazines, I was still in the broke pseudo celebrity category. Kirk could walk away from this photo shoot with millions to fall back on, from being a top basketball superstar, but I on the other hand needed all the exposure I could get. As much as this entire ordeal was working my nerves, getting the cover of this magazine would give me the boost I desperately needed right about now. If I had to beyond humble myself in order to make it happen, so be it.

"Excuse me, can we have a second?" I asked the photographer, who then looked over at Natalie. She nodded her head at him and then he gave me the okay. Honestly, neither of them had a choice if there was even a tiny chance we could make this work.

"I don't have anything to say to you," Kirk spit, before I had a chance to say one word to him.

"I know you don't like me, but I'm here, so let's make this work."

"Why? Because you're on the outs with your cheating boyfriend and you need another way to garner some publicity? Sorry, I'm not gonna let you use me to get it."

"Regardless of how you feel about my relationship with Skee, I'm here doing a job. When you met me, I was trying to pursue an acting career, so don't pretend that I'm some fame whore with no talent, trying to use you for a come up. In my line of business, do I need all the exposure I can get? Most definitely, but I have much bigger goals than being just arm candy."

"I thought you did, but you seemed more interested in running behind Skee than pursuing your own goals."

"That's where you're wrong. The reason Skee and I fell out is because I got a movie role, but instead of me taking it, he wanted me to go on tour with him. But I chose my career over, how did you put it, running behind Skee. So, have I made some mistakes, yeah, I've never claimed to be perfect. But I want my acting career to take off and that's why I'm here today, dealing with your bullshit. I'm doing my best to build my own name, so I can eventually make something of myself.

But like you told me, it takes time and a lot of hard work. So, I'm asking you—actually, I'm begging you— please, don't mess this up for me. If only for the next few hours, put aside the disgust you have for me and let's give them the mind-blowing photos they want."

Kirk's stare was so blank, I couldn't get a read if he was going to step up or let me drown. Without saying a word, he simply walked off and stood in position, being photo ready. I said a quick "please, help me" prayer in my head and decided to give it another try.

Diamond

"Diamond, you look gorgeous. So well-rested and tanned."

"Don't I! If only I could stay this dark all year long. And I should look rested. All Cameron and I did was stay laid up next to each other. Rather, it was in the bed, by our private pool or beach. All we did was relax. I wouldn't be surprised if we made a baby on our honeymoon," I laughed.

"You think so?"

"Anything is possible, but I doubt it."

"Why do you say that?"

"Because that would've made the trip too good to be true."

"Does that mean you're ready to have another baby?"

"Of course!" Diamond gushed.

"I love that man, so much. I couldn't imagine my life without him in it. Brining his child into this world would mean everything to me."

"I can honestly say I've never seen you this happy before."

"I've never been this happy. After the hell and

heartache Rico put me through, I really thought all men were pieces of shit. But Cameron, he's different. He's unlike any other man I've ever met and the crazy part is, he loves me."

"Diamond, why wouldn't he love you? You're a wonderful mother and amazing friend, with a heart of gold. Any man would be lucky to have you."

"I appreciate you saying that but..." my voice trailed off, as I thought about the fact that I was a recently reformed drug dealer, potential killer, and what many would consider a shady character.

"But what?"

"I've made some bad decisions in my life."

"Who hasn't? But unlike most people, you're always trying to help others. Trust me, Cameron knows how lucky he is to have you, that's why he put a ring on it."

"Kennedy, you always know the right thing to say. I guess that's why you're so successful when it comes to this PR thing."

"I appreciate that, darling, but I'm only speaking the truth. But, speaking of PR, while we're here enjoying our delicious lunch at the Four Seasons, our client Blair is probably having a hissy fit."

"Oh gosh, should I even ask why she would be having a hissy fit?" I questioned, reluctant to hear the answer.

"Well, I kinda set some things in motion, that I knew Blair wouldn't approve of."

"'Some things' like what?"

"A couple weeks ago, somebody that I'm cool with casually mentioned that Kirk had a photo shoot coming up for a potential magazine cover. I thought nothing of it at the time, but after a chat with Blair recently, I thought she might be perfect for the gig."

"Why would you think that, since Kirk pretty much hates Blair?"

"Because she's tempted to go back to Skee, and as our client we're supposed to do what's in her best interest. Blair running back to Skee is in nobody's best interest."

"So, what did you do?"

"I called in a major favor and had the magazine replace the model they had for the shoot, and use Blair instead."

"Are you serious!"

"They were actually thrilled to get her. They had some no name, low budget booty model lined up, but when I mentioned Blair they were psyched."

"Forget about them, what about Blair? You remember how cold Kirk was towards Blair when we saw him at that restaurant. Plus, Cameron told me that Kirk saw Blair at that party with Skee, and he was livid. Kirk told Cameron he wanted nothing to do with Blair."

"All that may be true, but I rather Blair rekindle things with Kirk than Skee."

"Rekindle! Kirk isn't going to rekindle anything. I wouldn't be surprised if he walked off the set."

"Don't say that. This would be a good look for *our* client," Kennedy stressed. "Just because you're a married woman now, don't forget you have another partner, too," she winked.

"Funny, but you know I'm excited about diving

into our business venture. That still doesn't change the fact that I don't know if throwing Blair and Kirk together was the right move. What if the photo shoot goes to hell? I guess you didn't think about that."

"Blair is a professional. She's going to make sure she gets the job done."

"I'm not worried about Blair getting the job done, I'm more concerned about Kirk shutting the shit down."

"You think he would do that?" Kennedy got this frazzled look on her face like this was the first time that had crossed her mind.

"You clearly don't know Kirk. He's a cool guy but he does have some of those same ego-driven traits that a lot of men suffer from. So, I wouldn't be surprised if he demanded another model for the shoot."

"Now, I feel horrible. Blair would be mortified if he did that to her. Maybe we should go over there."

"I'm not going over there. You created that nightmare," I said, putting my hand up. "I want no parts of that."

"I don't blame you. I'm going over there. If things go bad, I don't want Blair to have to deal with it by herself."

"I think that's a good idea."

"Are you sure you don't want to come?" Kennedy asked, in a begging tone.

"I'm positive! But we are partners, plus Blair is like my sister and I definitely don't want anybody messing with her, so fine, I'll come."

"You're the best...let's go!"

As I was grabbing my purse, so I could leave out

with Kennedy, I felt my phone vibrating non-stop. I finally reached inside for it, thinking it was Cameron. When I saw it was coming from an unknown number I declined to answer, but the caller wouldn't stop.

"Hold on a sec, Kennedy. Let me see who keeps blowing up my phone. Hello," I answered abruptly.

"I need to see you now."

"Who is this?" I snapped.

"Excuse me," the male said calmly but with much authority dripping from his tone and I instantly realized who was on the other end.

"My fault. I didn't recognize your voice at first. Can we meet in a couple hours? I was just headed out to handle some important business."

"It'll have to wait. My business with you comes first. I'll see you here shortly, at our usual spot." Before I could say another word he hung up.

"Kennedy, I'm sorry I have to do this to you, but that was my attorney and he needs to see me ASAP."

"Is everything okay?"

"Yeah, I just need to sign some paperwork."

"I wish you could come with me, but I can take care of this Blair situation on my own. Go handle your business and I'll call you later to let you know how everything went."

"Cool."

As I watched Kennedy walk away, I shook my head, dreading what was awaiting me.

Kennedy

When I arrived at the photo shoot, it looked completed deserted. There wasn't a soul in sight and I felt this sickness in the pit of my stomach. *Fuck! Diamond was probably right. Kirk made them cancel the shoot because he refused to work with Blair. Let me call her. She's probably furious*, I thought to myself, as I reached for my phone.

"Kennedy, I wasn't expecting to see you here," I heard someone call out," as I was about to dial Blair's number. I looked up to see who was talking to me and welcomed the familiar face.

"Hey, Natalie! It's good to see you," I smiled, hoping she had good news for me. "How did everything go?"

"A complete disaster," she revealed in a tone that was the exact opposite of her normal perky voice. But when it came down to serious business, Natalie always switched it up.

Shit! Fuck! Damn! I can't believe I ruined this, I screamed to myself.

"I'm so sorry, Natalie. I know how important this

photo shoot was for you. I should've..."

"Why are you sorry? It's not your fault the ceiling cracked and there's a terrible leak. You don't see the buckets over there?" She said, pointing to the puddles of water in the far corner.

"Oh gosh! That is terrible. So, you had to cancel the shoot?"

"We were going to, but luckily we found out there is an amazing rooftop pool. And we just got word that the owner of the building is going to allow us to use it, at no additional cost. So, it started off as a complete disaster but now we're good."

That's awesome!"

"Yeah, I just came down to get a couple of things that we needed. What brings you here?"

"I was coming to check on Blair."

"Blair, oh she's a friend of yours?"

"She's actually my client."

"I had no idea. You should've better prepared your client. She had no idea this was for our swim edition."

"Really, I didn't know that either."

"You didn't know what you got her booked for?"

"It all happened so fast and very last minute. How is the photo shoot going, now that you've found an alternate location?" I asked, wanting to move on to another subject.

"Honestly, that was almost a disaster too, but your client handled it very well."

"What happened?"

"You probably didn't know this, but Kirk McKnight is also doing the photo shoot with Blair. Clearly, they have history because Mr. McKnight wanted no parts of it."

"Get out, I wonder why?" I questioned, acting as if I was completely dumbfounded.

"I have no idea. But he wanted us to replace Blair as the model and she was willing to do so."

"Did you?"

"No! I was thrilled when I first found out she was being used as the model. I mean, with all that Skee Patron drama surrounding her, I thought it would be great for business. Plus, she's never done a photo shoot like this before. But Kirk McKnight is a superstar and he has a lot of pull, so I told Blair to do her best to get Kirk to cooperate."

"Was she able to get him to do it?"

"It's been difficult. Whatever bad blood is between them, it must run deep. When the ceiling started leaking, Kirk almost seemed relieved, as if he thought the shoot would have to be canceled. I have no idea how things are going now. But as hot as I think they look together, if Kirk doesn't loosen up, then we might have to replace Blair. I know that's the last thing you want to hear about your client."

"Do you mind if I go upstairs with you and observe the photo shoot? Just in case things go from bad to worse, I want to be there for my client."

"Of course you can come upstairs. Blair has been holding it together, but I'm sure she could use the additional support."

As I followed Natalie to the elevator, so we could go to the rooftop, I kept thinking about my conversation with Diamond. I made a bad call and now Blair was suffering for it. The last thing I wanted was for her to be embarrassed by Kirk. I had no idea he was the type to hold grudges.

"Come, sit over here," Natalie suggested. "That way, they won't see you until they take a break."

"When will that be?" I asked, anxious to speak to Blair.

"Shortly," she said, holding up two other swimsuits. "It's almost time for Blair to change."

"Cool."

I sat down and watched from a distance as the photo shoot took place. Natalie was correct: the scenery of the rooftop pool was beautiful. Unfortunately, she was also correct about the interaction between Kirk and Blair, it was painfully clear Kirk didn't want to be there. From the angle and distance I was sitting, I couldn't get a perfectly clear view but from what I could see, it seemed that Blair was trying to give cover ready poses, but Kirk was just standing like a statue. A flawless, chiseled statue, but lifeless.

"Outfit change," the photographer called out. He was probably ready to move on and get this over with, and I couldn't blame him. Most photographers had no problem talking shit to models, but when dealing with high profile celebrities it was a different story. They didn't feel comfortable telling stars that their photos sucked and to step it up. Not only was Kirk McKnight a celebrity, but with his height and build, a very intimidating one.

I immediately stood up and waved my hand at Blair, when she began walking away from where they were shooting. It took me a minute to get her attention because she had her head down, as if defeated.

"Kennedy, I'm so glad to see you," she sighed, once we were face to face. "Talk about a photo shoot from hell."

"At least you look gorgeous," I said, trying in vain to change her frown into a smile.

"Natalie, can you give us a couple minutes?" I asked, when I saw her approaching.

"Sure thing."

"I'm sure Natalie and everybody else is regretting they ever hired me for this photo shoot. But it's not my fault. If they had told you I would be working with Kirk, I know you would've politely declined. Instead they kept the shit under wraps and now I'm in the most fucked up position, and feeling like a complete loser."

"Blair, you're not a loser. Who would have ever guessed Kirk would act so unprofessional? I mean damn, all he has to do is pose with a hot girl. What's so fuckin' hard about that."

"Yeah, but that hot girl happens to be me and to him I'm not so hot."

"I'll take care of it."

"What are you going to do?"

"Place a phone call and come up with some sort of reason why you need to be excused from the set ASAP. I'll figure it out."

"You want me to quit?"

"You're not quitting, Blair. It's not right that you've been put in this position and I want to make it right for you. You're my client and it's my job."

"Kennedy, I appreciate that, but even after begging

Kirk to help make this photo shoot successful, I'm still not ready to give up."

"I admire the fact you want to push through this torment, but Kirk has shaded you enough."

"Let me give it one last try."

"Why, so he can try to make you feel worse than you already do? You don't deserve that and I feel horrible for even being a part of this."

"Don't feel horrible. It's not your fault they didn't tell you about Kirk."

"That's the thing, they..."

"Kennedy, just stop." Blair put her hand up, cutting me off before I could tell her the truth. That I'm the one responsible for putting her in this fucked up position. "You always get me out of messes, let me get myself out of this one. Trust me, I can do this. I have to go change swimsuits but stay close. Having you here does mean a lot to me."

Blair gave me a kiss on the cheek and walked off towards Natalie, before I could get another word out. With the emotional yoyo Blair had been on for the last few months, I regretted that I was now guilty of adding to it. I should've minded my own business and stayed out of her relationship with Skee. With all my maneuvering, after this epic fail, Blair was probably going to go right back to him, anyway.

Blair

While the photographer was making some adjustments with the lighting, I stood off to the side, observing Kirk. He was still giving off the same negative vibes, guaranteeing this photo shoot would be a complete wash. But I had come so far in less than a year, and I refused to let him ruin all the progress Kennedy and I had made with my career. One thing I was learning quickly in this business was that you rarely get opportunities. If you're one of the lucky ones that do, you better seize the moment, because more than likely it won't come again.

Begging Kirk to cooperate clearly didn't work, so I had to come up with a new strategy. That meant trying to get into his psyche and what brought out the kind person in him. I knew Kirk had it in him, because he showed me his soft side on several occasions. I quickly thought back to all the intimate conversations we shared, where we both revealed some of our deepest feelings. My heart was pounding because time wasn't on my side and I had to come up with a game plan quick.

"Blair, would you feel comfortable standing on this while posing?" the photographer questioned, pointing to an odd shaped figurine.

"Sure," I replied, somewhat reluctantly. I surmised that in a desperate attempt to save this photo shoot, the photographer was pulling out props. Probably hoping it would make it less obvious that Kirk had no desire to be there.

"Thank goodness," I heard him say under his breath, as if in stress. The photographer seemed to have given up on giving Kirk any suggestions on how to pose and instead focused on me. I was doing my best to comply, when an idea struck me. I wasn't sure if it would work, but it was worth a try.

"You're doing great, Blair. Can you turn this way, and lift your arm towards Kirk," the photographer directed.

Here goes nothing, I thought to myself, before I did my best fake fall in Kirk's direction. *Please, let Kirk react like the gentleman I know he is and not let me fall flat on my face,* I prayed to myself before throwing my body in his direction, as if slipping on the figurine.

"Aaah!" I shrieked, upon my downfall. I heard what sounded like Kennedy call out my name in concern, as others seemed to scramble towards me. But just like I prayed, Kirk was my savior. His strong, muscular arms swept me up for the save, right on time, as if it had been scripted.

"Blair, are you okay?" he asked, with so much concern in his eyes, that I almost felt guilty for staging this little ruse.

"I think I am," I said, in a breathless voice. I put my acting chops to work and conjured up the look of fear across my face.

"Let me sit you down over here," Kirk said, carrying me over to a chaise lounge chair. "Does this hurt?" he asked, gently touching parts of my leg to make sure I didn't sprain anything.

"Oh my goodness, Blair, are you okay? My heart dropped when I saw you falling."

"I'm fine. Thanks to Kirk. Thank you so much for catching me before I fell. I'm so embarrassed."

"Don't be embarrassed. It's my fault. If I hadn't been acting like such a jerk, that photographer would've never put you on that stupid thing. I'm just glad you're okay," Kirk said, putting his head down, trying to hide his guilt-ridden face.

"It's okay," I smiled, giving Kennedy a wink on the sly. Her eyes widened in surprise, clearly shocked by my antics. But hell, a girl has to do what a girl has to do, when her back is against the wall.

"Blair, I apologize for asking you to pose up there. I should've known it could be dangerous," the photographer admitted. Are you okay to continue?"

"I'm fine. I can continue, if Kirk is up to it." He was still kneeling down, so I put my hand under his chin and lifted his face up. "Are you?"

"Definitely. Let's do this and let's do it right." Kirk stood up and took my hand. "Do you need me to carry you?"

"I think I got it, but it would be helpful if I could lean on you."

"Of course."

I turned my head back and gave Kennedy a smile before walking off holding on to Kirk. I might have been smiling on the outside, but on the inside I was breathing a sigh of relief. I finally had faith that we might get that front cover status after all.

Diamond

When I arrived to meet Renny, he was wrapping up a phone call that seemed to be putting him in a bad mood. I was hoping it was only temporary, because a bad mood mixed with Renny's already callous attitude wasn't a pleasant combination.

"What took you so long to get here?" were the first words out of Renny's mouth, when he ended his phone call.

"I got here as soon as I could. The Friday traffic didn't help. So, what was so urgent?"

"Come on, I need you to take a ride with me," Renny stated, grabbing his keys.

"Where are we going?"

"We'll discuss it when we get in the car."

I let out a deep sigh, realizing this wasn't going to be a short visit. I wondered if I should text Cameron and let him know I would be home later on, but decided against it. If I sent him a text, that would probably lead to him calling me and I didn't want to have a conversation with him in front of Renny.

"How's Nichelle?" I asked casually, thinking that

mentioning his wife would lighten the mood. But instead of responding, Renny simply got in the car and shut the door. We were driving for thirty minutes, before Renny said a word.

"I had to terminate the services of the worker I brought in to replace you, permanently. I recruited somebody from the west coast and I need you to train him on how to run your old territory."

"Why me?"

"Because when you ran it, I had no issues and I can't afford any more fuck ups. I'm losing a lot of money over some bullshit and that needs to be dead. We're on our way to meet the new worker now and I want you to break him in properly."

"Renny, I'm a married woman now. I told you months ago that I was putting my old life behind me."

"Was that before or after I saved your life when Parish was about to kill you? And let's not forget about Darcy. Or that coma your baby's father woke up from temporarily and you begged me to make sure it didn't happen again. I don't think your new husband would be so forgiving if he knew you were the one who shot Rico and that's why your daughter has been without her dad. Me personally, I think Rico got exactly what he deserved for setting you up, but I don't know if your Superstar NBA husband will be so understanding."

I gazed out the window as I listened to what Renny said. I was still in the honeymoon stage of my marriage and had to deal with this fuckery. In my mind I had created this fantasy, that once I said "I do" all my sins would be left in the past. How naive of me.

"Renny, I want to help you, but…"

"There are no 'buts', Diamond. I told you the first time you came to me to fix your problem that you better be prepared to step up, when I needed you to do something for me. That time has come."

"How long do you think this is gonna take?"

"It's your old territory, you tell me. But don't half-ass it. I need the shit done right."

"This west coast dude, where on the totem pole is he, as far as how fast he learns."

"He was my best worker on the west coast, that's why I'm bringing him in. But we both know the game works a little different over here."

"True, but if he listens and follows directions, he'll be operating the territory smoothly, without any hiccups." At least, that was what I prayed for. I couldn't afford to invest a lot of time into this, but I also had to make sure this new worker didn't fuck up. If he didn't perform up to par, the wrath of Renny wouldn't be pretty.

♥

"Hey, baby! I brought some goodies," I smiled, holding a takeout bag from Cameron's favorite Indian restaurant.

"As much as I love that food, I am much happier to see my wife," Cameron said, giving me a long, passionate kiss. "I've been calling you, but you weren't answering your phone. Where have you been?"

"I had lunch with Kennedy earlier and left my phone at the restaurant. By the time I realized I didn't have it, I was all the way at my mother's house."

"Did you get it back?"

"Finally. I just got it back right before I came home."

"I might have to install a GPS on you. I don't like not being able to find my wife."

"I love when you call me that. Say it again."

"My wife. My wife...my wife...my wife," Cameron kept repeating, as he unbuttoned my blouse.

"Do you know how turned on I get, every time you say that?"

"Tell me how turned on you get."

"It makes me want to do this," I said, kneeling down and unzipping Cameron's jeans. I pulled down his boxer shorts and covered the tip of his dick with my moist lips, until getting each inch wetter and wetter.

"Damn, baby," Cameron moaned, as he tilted his back, while stroking my hair. At this moment, bringing my husband pleasure made up for the pain I felt for the non-stop lies I continued to tell.

Kennedy

"Girl, I have to give you props. Not only did I think your fall was legitimate, but I didn't even think you were slick enough to fake some shit like that," I chuckled.

"It's called desperation. That man had me scrambling for an idea. I'm just glad that I came up with one that worked."

"So am I. But I'm more relieved that Kirk was there to catch you. Blair, if you would've busted your ass or fell on your face, I'd been devastated."

"Hell...me too! But it all worked out."

"It beyond worked out. I got a call from Natalie today and they got their cover shot. So, cheers to you," I grinned, raising my glass.

"Unbelievable. I so needed some great news... thank you!"

"Don't thank me. You deserve the credit for making this happen. I was ready to throw in the towel and have you walk off the set, but you refused. I don't give you enough credit. You're a fighter, Blair."

"Maybe some of your attributes are rubbing off on me."

"I like the sound of that."

"Well, let me say something else that I'm sure will sound good to you."

"Do tell," I said, raising an eyebrow.

"Kirk and I are going out on a date tonight."

"Seriously?"

"Yep. He called me the other day and we had a great conversation. So great that I've decided not to return Skee's calls or his text messages."

"Good girl!" I cheered, clapping my hands. "This day is just getting better and better."

"I was confident that bit of news would be music to your ears."

"Of course it is. Personally, I think Kirk is a much better fit for you than Skee ever was."

"We'll see what happens. But, let me go. I'm taking this new acting class and if you're even one minute late the teacher locks the door and won't let you in. He's a complete asshole, but a phenomenal acting coach. Gotta go," Blair said, grabbing her purse before rushing out.

I couldn't help but smile with admiration, watching Blair make her exit. After all her drama with Skee, she finally seemed to be getting her spark back. For a little while, Blair had me worried that might not ever happen, but luckily she was proving me wrong.

"Hey! Sorry I'm late," Diamond waved as she walked up to the table. "I saw Blair damn near running out the door when I was coming in."

"Yeah, she's taking a new acting class and being late isn't an option."

"Good for Blair. I'm glad that even though she's

getting work, she's still trying to improve her craft."

"Yep and not only is she trying to improve her professional life, she's also doing the same with her personal one."

"Coming from you, that can only mean she hasn't gone back to Skee."

"That would be correct. I will say, you were right. Kirk gave Blair hell initially, but it all worked out and they're going on a date tonight. So, good riddance Skee."

"Congrats, your plan worked out."

"Yes, it did. Before I forget, Cameron called the office earlier today looking for you."

"Oh yeah, I spoke to him."

"He was under the impression you were gonna be in the office. It would've been nice if he was right."

"No need to be catty."

"I'm just saying. We're partners in this business but for the last few days you've been a ghost. If you're not with your husband, what's going on with you?"

"A problem has come up with a friend of mine and they need my help. I don't want Cameron to know about it, so I've been telling him I'm at the office. I would appreciate if you would cover for me."

"Of course, you know I have your back."

"Thank you."

"But I have to tell you. It makes me a little concerned that you're a newlywed and you're already keeping secrets from your husband. That's not exactly a good way to start off a marriage."

"Kennedy, you're my girl, but unless I ask you for marital advice, please don't give it."

"Say no more. Enough about your marriage, let's discuss business. We just got hired to not only do the PR for an upcoming event, but they also want us to plan it. And it pays very well."

"That's awesome! Who is it for?"

"A new, high-end makeup line. They want to go all out for the launch. The budget is ridiculous. They already have a couple of models they'll be using as the faces of the product, but wouldn't it be amazing if we could get Blair a spot."

"That would be beyond amazing. Do you think it's a real possibility?"

"I do. I just have to find the right way to position my proposition. You catch that," I giggled at my word usage.

"You're so silly, but I have no doubt you'll be able to maneuver it."

"Thanks for your vote of confidence. But Diamond, this is a huge catch and can lead to even bigger projects. So, I'm going to need your help. I can't do this alone."

"I know and I promise you I won't let you down. But realistically, I'm going to need a few more days to help my friend out. Once I get that taken care of, you'll have my full attention."

"That works. I'm also going to bring in Tiffany to assist us and hire a couple of other people, too. With the budget they're giving us, we can afford to get some additional help."

"Wow, our company's first major event, this is exciting. Wait until I tell Cameron."

"I have to admit, I'm excited too. I've done a ton of

events, but Darcy was always the person that benefitted from it. For this to be ours, it's an incredible feeling. Maybe I'll finally start getting the respect as a real mover and shaker in this business."

"Kennedy, you will because it's long overdo. You've put in the work and it's time for people in this industry to take notice."

"I won't argue with that. We're going to pull every A-Lister in town and make this the best makeup launch this city has ever seen!"

Blair

"Did I tell you how beautiful you look tonight?"

"As a matter of fact, you did, when you first picked me up. But you're more than welcome to tell me again."

"You look beautiful."

"Thank you, Mr. Kirk McKnight. You told me to wear something extra nice tonight, although I still have no clue where you're taking me."

"To a movie premiere. I knew you would want to be red carpet ready."

"Are you sure I look okay?"

"Didn't I tell you twice how beautiful you look?"

"Yeah, but this is regular beautiful not red carpet. I didn't even have a professional do my makeup. I wish you would have told me. Cameras can be so cruel."

"Blair, you're perfect," Kirk said, trying to reassure me.

"If I look like crap on those blogs tomorrow, I'm blaming you."

"Trust me, you have nothing to worry about. You'll be the most beautiful woman there. I promise you."

"You always know the right thing to say to me. It's

been that way since the first time we met."

"You make it easy."

"I do?"

"Yes. Even when I was pissed at you, I was still happy to see you."

"Maybe you need to go into acting because you totally had me fooled. I thought for sure you would rather be anywhere but next to me."

"I didn't want to let you back in, so I figured I needed to shut you completely out."

"Yeah, you made it pretty impossible for me to breakthrough. But thank goodness you have a heart."

"I couldn't let you fall."

"You never do," I said, before leaning in and kissing Kirk.

"Our night together is just beginning and it's already perfect."

"Just wait until we get to the end," I teased.

"Mr. McKnight, we're here," the driver said, stopping the SUV in front of the venue.

"Are you ready?"

"Sure am." When we stepped out of the SUV holding hands, the cameras instantly started flashing. It seemed no matter how many red carpets I walked; I always got butterflies in my stomach. The nervousness never seemed to let up.

Although my face wasn't beat or my hair wasn't laid the way I would've preferred, since I was going to be in the spotlight. Luckily, I was wearing a gold Herve Leger bandage dress that always photographed well. I smiled, waved, and gave my best face possible. Although most of the photos were taken with Kirk and I together, it felt good when a lot of the photographers wanted pics of me, by myself. That was a sign that I was finally developing a name of my own.

By the time we made our way inside, most of my nervousness had subsided. But I wanted to check my appearance, in case I needed a touch-up.

"Kirk, can you excuse me for a second. I need to use the restroom.

"Sure. I'll be right over there, talking to a friend of mine," he said pointing to a man that seemed to be getting interviewed.

"He looks familiar."

"Yeah, that's my homeboy, Marc Tye. He's the star of the movie. That's why I came to support. This is his first lead role."

"I've heard of him. That's incredible. I can't wait for my first leading lady role."

"It'll happen for you. Just wait and see."

"Thank you." I gave Kirk a brief kiss and headed to the restroom.

When I got to the bathroom, I was pleasantly surprised that only one person could utilize it at a time. That meant I had complete privacy to try and doll myself up, without being disturbed. To guarantee no interruptions, I walked over to lock the door when suddenly the door flung open.

"I see you wearing the dress that I got you."

"Skee, what are you doing here?" My heart was racing. I hadn't seen Skee in the flesh in what seemed like forever.

"Since you stopped takin' my calls, when I saw you here, I decided to take advantage of the opportunity."

"This isn't a good time."

"Why, 'cause you here wit' that basketball nigga?"

"That and we're in the bathroom. Somebody could walk in."

"We can easily take care of that," he said, locking the door.

"What do you want?"

"What I always wanted...you."

"That's not gonna happen."

"We seemed to be makin' progress. The last time we talked you even said you were ready to give it another try. Then you stopped takin' my calls or responding to my text. What the fuck happened?"

"I changed my mind."

"You changed your mind or you got some new dick?"

"How dare you. Even though I haven't had sex with Kirk yet, even if I did, it's none of your fuckin' business."

"You here wit' the next nigga, wearing a dress I bought you, and it's none of my business."

"Really, Skee. A dress...if I had something else to put on, I would take this shit off and hand it right back to you."

"Fuck you and that dress. If you wanna be wit' that basketball nigga, then so be it." Skee stormed out the bathroom, leaving me shaking my head. I didn't understand what the fuck just happened.

"The ending of that movie blew my mind. I wasn't expecting any of that to happen," I commented to Kirk, when we got back in the SUV.

"Me neither. Tye did the damn thing. I think he has a box office hit with that one."

"No doubt. This will definitely not be his last leading role."

"For sure. So, are you up to hitting the after party?"

"Not really."

"I wasn't gonna say anything, but I saw Skee. Could you not wanting to go to the party have to do with him?"

"No, that has nothing to do with it."

"You don't have to lie to me. I know the breakup still might be hard for you and seeing him tonight could've put you in a foul mood."

"I'm good. I had such a great time with you tonight."

"Then what is it? It's still early. Why do you want the night to end?"

"Who said anything about the night being over?"

"But you just said you didn't want to go to the party."

"I don't. I would rather us have our own private party. I mean, if that's okay with you."

"Are you saying you want to go back to my place?"

"That's exactly what I'm saying."

"'Say no more....back to my crib," Kirk directed the driver, before taking my hand.

When we arrived at Kirk's duplex penthouse on Hudson Street, I immediately fell in love with the place. The entire unit rests on an Art Deco building, in New York's swanky Tribeca. You were completely surrounded by glass, with 360-degree panoramic views of Manhattan and the Hudson River.

"This place is breathtaking," I said, staring out one of the many windows. There was even a glass staircase inside.

"Thank you."

"How long have you lived here?"

"Almost a year. I bought it when I resigned with the team. It was a gift to myself for my new contract."

"Some gift," I smiled.

"Can I get you something to drink?" Kirk asked, turning on some melodic music. I was tempted to tell him that there was no need for music. Just standing in a place like this would put anybody in the mood to make passionate love.

"No, thanks, I'm fine. I have everything I need."

"I hope that means me," Kirk said, as he came closer, reaching his hand out to me. I nodded my head and took his hand. I smiled in anticipation, as Kirk led me to his bedroom. I felt like some sort of goddess walking up the glass stairs. I didn't even know a staircase like this existed. Midway up the stairs, I stopped for a second and took off my shoes. With the open spaces between each stair, I got nervous that I would trip and fall in my six-inch heels.

When we got to the top of the stairs, the hallway leading to the bedroom appeared to be completely white crystal glass and the floor was heated. This was definitely every single man and woman's dream pad.

When I stepped in Kirk's bedroom, before I could even say a word, his lips were pressed against mine and our tongues were intertwined. Between kisses we undressed each other, in an almost animalistic way. You would've thought neither of us had sex in like, forever, the way we couldn't keep our hands off each other. Well, it had been months for me, but I'm sure the same couldn't be said for Kirk. I think our passion reflected this buildup we created, by taking so long to give into our mutual attraction for each other.

Once we were both naked, Kirk lifted me up off my feet and carried me over to his bed. After laying me down, his once aggressive lust turned into gentle lovemaking. His soft full lips began sprinkling my body with inviting kisses. My erected nipples tingled at the touch of Kirk's wet mouth. As my body became his playground, I craved to feel Kirk inside of me.

"I want you so bad," Kirk said, in a low voice as our eyes locked.

"I want you too." Right after I said those words, Kirk filled my insides up. I was so wet, but still felt a painful pressure, due to Kirk's massive tool. Luckily, he kept his strokes slow but steady, as if to allow my walls to adjust to his size. Kirk was a considerate lover, which made our first time even more pleasurable. That night we made love over and over again, until we finally fell asleep in each other's arms.

When I woke up in the morning, Kirk's arms were still wrapped around me. I felt so secure and content next to him, that I closed my eyes and went back to sleep.

But before I dozed off, I could hear Kirk waking up. He leaned over and kissed my forehead, before carefully freeing me from his arms. I figured he must've thought I was still asleep and didn't want to wake me. While he walked to the bathroom, I opened my eyes and I got a glimpse of his naked body. Even in the daylight, Kirk's physique was flawless.

Once Kirk was in the bathroom and I heard the shower running, I sat up and smiled. I found myself blushing, like I was in junior high with a schoolgirl crush. He had me feeling all giddy inside and I loved it. As I began replaying every wonderful moment of last night's sex session, I heard a text message coming through on my iPhone. I reached over on the dresser and grabbed my purse. I saw a few text messages from Kennedy, but the most recent was from Skee. At first I tossed my phone down, not wanting to read anything he said, but my curiosity got the best of me.

I want to apologize for last night. I was out of line. If you want to move on, I have to accept that, but could we at least meet and talk, so we can both get closure

I re-read Skee's text over and over again. This sadness came over me thinking that this could really be the end of our relationship. As much as Skee hurt me, I couldn't lie to myself and pretend that I still didn't have strong feelings for him. I knew he wasn't the right man for me; plus, I genuinely liked Kirk and wanted to see where our relationship could go. But I wouldn't be able to do that until I dealt with the unresolved feelings I had for Skee.

Sure, we can meet and talk.

Can you meet me @ Megu in Midtown 1:00?

I looked up at the top of my phone to see what time it was. I had enough time to get home, change, and meet Skee at that time.

I'll be there.
See you then

"Oh gosh, you startled me," I jumped, when I noticed Kirk standing in the doorway, with a towel wrapped around his waist.

"Sorry about that. I thought you were still asleep. Is everything okay?" he asked, looking down as I was tightly gripping my phone.

"I'm fine. I was just going back and forth with Kennedy on text," I lied. I didn't want to ruin how great last night was for us by bringing up Skee. "How long have you been up?" I asked, although I already knew the answer, but I wanted to divert the conversation in another direction.

"Not that long. I would've asked you to join me in the shower, but you looked so peaceful sleeping, so I decided not to disturb you."

"That was thoughtful of you, but next time wake me up. I would much rather be in the shower with you, than in this bed alone."

"Who said there's gonna be a next time," Kirk replied, with a devilish grin on his face.

"Oh, so you've put me in the one night stand groupie category," I shot back, throwing a pillow at him.

"Never that," he said, quickly coming towards me before nuzzling my neck. Kirk's nuzzling turned to kisses and that's all it took for me to want him inside of me again. "You're going to make me late for practice," Kirk said, as he had now worked his kisses down to my shoulder.

"I'll be worth it...I promise," I whispered in his ears, as he dropped his towel and got back under the blanket with me.

❤

By the time Kirk and I finished making love and he dropped me off at my apartment, I had hardly any time to get ready to meet Skee. I sent him a text letting him know I would be late, but I knew he was pissed. Skee expected everyone to wait on him, but demanded promptness from others.

I took a quick shower, pulled my hair in a bun, threw on a wrap dress, applied some lip-gloss, grabbed my purse, and caught a cab. During my ride to the restaurant, my mind kept flipping between Kirk and Skee. Both men were so different, yet something about them seemed almost the same to me, but I couldn't put my finger on it.

After I paid the cab driver and entered Megu, the hostess came right over to me and took me directly to

Skee's table. It seemed as if she had been waiting for my arrival.

"Glad you finally made it," Skee said casually, as he stood up and kissed me on the cheek. I had to admit, I was surprised how calm he was, especially since I was about 20 minutes late.

"I apologize for being late. I know how much you detest tardiness."

"No worries. Are you hungry? Because I already ordered for you."

"Actually I am hungry and thanks. Is this drink mine?"

"Yes. I had the waitress bring you a Bellini, since that's what you normally get. Is that fine or did you want something else?"

"No, this is perfect. I need a drink," I said nervously, as I took a sip from the champagne glass.

"Again, I want to apologize for last night. I shouldn't have confronted you in the bathroom. It was inappropriate."

"I can't believe you're apologizing to me. This is so not like you."

"Believe it or not I'm trying to do better."

"Really, what brought that on?"

"You. I messed up a good thing between us and if there is any chance we can make it work, I want us to try."

"I thought we were meeting to get closure, not about us getting back together."

"Is that what you really want? For it to be over between us." When I was about to respond, the servers brought out our food and I stayed quiet until they left. But before I said a word, I guzzled down my drink, hoping for liquor courage.

"Skee, I'm going to be honest with you. Part of me doesn't want to let go, but I know it's the best thing for me."

"Why is that the best thing for you? Are you saying you weren't happy with me?"

"I was happy with you, but I think I got too caught up in your world and started forgetting who I was. Then when you cheated on me..." My voice trailed off as I put my head down. Even though that had happened months ago, it still hurt my heart every time I thought about it.

"Blair, I told you how sorry I was for what happened but it won't happen again."

"You can't promise me that. What happens next time when you want me to be somewhere and my work doesn't permit it? Are you then going to parade another woman in my face, to embarrass and humiliate me...I mean." I stopped mid sentence and put my hand on the temple of my head.

"Are you okay?"

"I'm fine. I think I finished my drink too fast. Having alcohol on an empty stomach is never good. I'm sure I'll feel better once I eat my food.

"Eat your food and we can finish discussing after you're done."

"Okay, but I can talk and eat," I laughed.

"Then answer this question for me, between bites."

"What is it?"

"Does your relationship with Mr. Basketball have anything to do with you not wanting to get back together with me?"

"I'm not going to lie to you and say that I don't have feelings for Kirk."

"So, is he your man now?"

"No, he isn't, but neither are you and that's your fault. It has nothing to do with Kirk. It's because you cheated on me."

"Can't we get past that?"

"I don't think I can. I feel like if I don't do exactly what you want, when you want me to, you will cheat again. I can't deal with that," I said, before grabbing my glass of water. "I feel so light headed."

"Do you need some more water?"

"Yeah, I do." Skee signaled to the waiter to bring some more water. While I waited for it to come, I ate some more of my food, thinking it would stop this dizziness coming over me.

"I think we need to go," Skee suggested.

"Maybe so. Something is off."

"Have my driver bring the car to the front. We'll be out shortly," Skee told the hostess. "Blair, do you need a ride home?"

"Yeah, that would be great. I don't know what's wrong with me."

"Like you said, drinking on an empty stomach then so quickly. It's probably just fuckin' wit' you. I'm sure you'll feel better, once you lay down."

"I'm sure you're right," I agreed, although my mind and body was saying something else. I followed

Skee out to the car, almost in a daze.

❤

When I woke up, I struggled to keep my eyes open. At first I couldn't focus and once I finally did, I realized I was naked. My eyes darted around the room and my surroundings looked familiar to me, but I wasn't sure.

"Where am I," I mumbled out loud, not expecting to get a response, because I thought I was alone.

"Sleeping beauty. You finally woke up." My heart jumped when I noticed Skee lying next to me in bed and he was naked, too. "Don't be scared, it's just me."

"What are we doing in bed together...naked?"

"You don't remember us coming back to my place an having makeup sex?"

"We had sex?" I asked, as my voice cracked.

"Of course and it was excellent."

I was speechless. I was trying to process what Skee said and none of it made any sense to me. How did I go from waking up in Kirk's bed this morning to being in Skee's bed the exact same day? This all seemed surreal to me and I had no idea what to do next.

Diamond

I woke up in a great mood. Mainly because I knew this was the last day that I would need to finish up the assignment Renny gave me. His new recruit was actually cool to work with, but I was sick of lying to Cameron. I was ready to put that life of crime behind me and focus on being a great wife, mother, and businesswoman. If all went well, this time tomorrow I would be waking up to just that.

Cameron wasn't in bed, so I figured he had already left for basketball practice. Destiny was at my mother's house and I couldn't wait to pick her up today. Lately, my mother wanted to keep Destiny all the time and I began to wonder if she was getting lonely. As I was thinking about fun things my mom could do to occupy her time, I went over to the dresser to get my phone. To my surprise, I had a ton of missed calls and text messages.

"What the hell is going on?" I asked out loud, as I scrolled through some of the text messages. Several were from Kennedy, saying it was urgent and I needed to call her ASAP. Right when I was about to dial her number I heard the front door slam shut. "Cameron, is that you?" I called out.

"Yeah," he yelled back. I was wondering did something go wrong at practice because his tone seemed off. I put my phone down and decided to check on Cameron before calling Kennedy back.

"Baby, is everything okay?" I asked, practically bumping into him in the hallway.

"You tell me," he shot back, holding up today's copy of the New York Post. "Who the fuck is this nigga!"

I swallowed hard and my heart sunk when I saw photos of me and the west coast dude Renny had me training together. "Cameron, it's not what you think."

"Then explain this shit to me. 'Cause from where I'm standing, this looks like my wife creeping wit' some other man."

"No, it's nothing like that."

"Then who is he, Diamond?"

"It's my cousin. He needed me to help him with some things. These photos aren't what they seem."

"Your cousin...huh? I thought I met all your family at our wedding. Why wasn't this family member there?"

"He lives on the west coast and couldn't make it."

"Is that right?"

"Yes."

"Okay, well get him on the phone, so I can speak to him. As a matter of fact, I'll call your mother and ask her about him. What's this cousin's name?" Cameron questioned, holding his phone to call my mother. My stomach was doing flips. I couldn't come up with lies fast enough to keep up with Cameron's questions. "What is his fuckin' name, Diamond!"

"Cameron, calm down and listen to me." Cameron's eyes were twitching and anger consumed his face. The walls seemed to be closing in on me and I didn't know how to respond. When I thought about all the scenarios that could go wrong with working for Renny, being splashed in the New York Post wasn't on the list. I kept on forgetting that I was married to not only one of the biggest basketball players in New York but also in the NBA.

"Don't tell me to calm down. The only thing I want coming out of your mouth is your cousin's name."

"I can't give you that."

"Why? Because he isn't your fuckin' cousin! 'Cause you fuckin' this nigga! We ain't even been married for a year and you cheating on me! What the fuck is wrong wit' you!" Cameron barked, tossing the newspaper in my face. I had never seen him so angry and it was freaking me the fuck out.

"I swear on everything that I haven't cheated on you. I would never cheat on you, Cameron. I love you so much. Our family means everything to me. I wouldn't ruin it by cheating on you. You have to believe me," I pleaded, as the tears streamed down my face.

"Then who the fuck is he? And I don't want any of your bullshit lies, Diamond. Either you tell me the truth or I'm walking out the door."

"He's a drug dealer from the west coast, that a man I used to work for and owed a favor to asked me to train. For the last few weeks, instead of going to the office like I said, I was training him to take over the drug operation that I used to run."

"Wait, you're telling me you used to be a drug dealer? Cut the bullshit, Diamond. I told you I wanted the truth."

"It is the truth," I admitted, burying my face in my hands. "I'm going to tell you the whole truth and it's ugly. But I rather you know this ugly truth than for you to ever believe I would ever let another man touch me besides you."

"I don't understand. Are you saying those drug charges that eventually got dropped, were true?"

"Yes."

"Does that have something to do with the favor you owed this guy you used to work with?"

"Yes. I went to him for help and he took care of it. And that time I went missing and you all thought I was dead; he was the one who saved my life. You have to understand, Cameron. Before and after I had Destiny, Rico treated me like shit. I was so insecure and my self-esteem was beaten. All I wanted to do was take care of my daughter and free myself from Rico. I turned to Renny for help."

"This is unreal. My wife is a drug dealer."

"An ex-drug dealer. I was so damaged after my relationship with Rico, that I never thought I would meet a man who I could trust enough to want to change my life. But when I met you, that all changed. We fell in love and I wanted to put that lifestyle behind me. "

"If you trusted me so much, then why didn't you come clean from the start?"

"Because I wasn't proud of the decisions I made and I didn't want to get you caught up in my mistakes."

"What about Rico?"

"What about him?"

"Did you shoot him? Are you responsible for him being in a coma like his girlfriend said?"

I hesitated for a moment before answering. I was afraid to tell the entire truth, but I was more afraid of losing my husband. "Yes, I did."

"Why?"

"Remember, when I moved in with my mother?"

"Yes?"

"I lied to you about the reason. It was actually because I was robbed at gunpoint in my bedroom. Rico found out I was making a lot of money selling drugs and he set me up. He let his friend rob me and even told him he could rape me, if he wanted to." My eyes watered up again as I thought about that night and my rage over that incident became fresh. "I wanted Rico dead for what he did to me."

Cameron stared at me and then turned around and walked off. I stood motionless for a few seconds, before following him into the living room. He was sitting down on the couch, looking up at the ceiling, as if in deep thought.

"I know this is a lot for you to deal with, but I'm glad you finally know the truth. Keeping these secrets from my husband was tearing me up inside."

"At least one of us feels better, because I'm more confused than ever. You're not the woman I thought I married. I don't know who you are."

"Cameron, I'm still Diamond. The person you fell in love with. You have to believe that," I said, kneeling on the floor beside him.

"I don't know. After this, I don't know if we can make this marriage work."

"Are you saying you want a divorce?" I stuttered asking the question, because I didn't want it to be true.

"I can't answer that question right now," Cameron said standing up.

"Baby, please don't give up on us. I love you, so much. I can't imagine my life without you in it. Please, forgive me." But my pleas seemed to fall on deaf ears, because the last thing I heard, was the front door slamming, after Cameron walked out on me.

Kennedy

"Diamond, I've been trying to get in touch with you all morning. How did you get pass all those reporters out front?

"I came in through the back way. I figured they would be posted up."

"I guess that means you've already seen the paper?"

"Yep, and so has my husband, or soon to be ex-husband."

"So, the story is true?" the shock in my voice was evident.

"Of course not! I would never cheat on Cameron."

"Then why would you be calling him your ex, as if the two of you are getting a divorce?"

"I admitted some things to him that I'm not sure he can get over."

"Things like what?"

"I don't want to talk about it."

"Must be pretty serious stuff."

"It is. I'm worried about my marriage, Kennedy. If Cameron leaves me..." Before Diamond could finish, she broke down and started sobbing. I had never seen her so fragile before and it broke my heart to see Diamond this way. She was always so strong that it was easy to forget that sometimes Diamond needed a shoulder to cry on, like anybody else.

"It's going to be okay. Cameron loves you and adores Destiny. He's not going to leave his family."

"I want to believe that, but if you could've seen the look in his eyes when he walked out on me."

"Come over here and sit down," I said, taking Diamond's hand. "Can I get you some water or juice?"

"I'll pass on a drink, unless it's something a lot stronger than water or juice."

"Hey, I can make it happen. There's a liquor store right around the corner," we both laughed.

"If only it was that easy to make the pain go away."

"Is that my phone or your phone that keeps ringing?" I asked, as the non-stop sound was annoying me."

"I think it's yours." I went over to my desk to check.

"Nope, it's not mine. It must be yours."

"Maybe it's Cameron calling," Diamond said, jumping up to get her phone. It started ringing again before she even reached it. "Hello. I couldn't make it today. You don't get the New York Post?" Diamond asked in a sarcastic tone.

It was obvious Diamond wasn't talking to Cameron, but whoever it was had her upset. I wish I could hear who was on the other end of the phone, but since I couldn't, I had to dissect the conversation the best I could, based off what Diamond was saying.

"You don't have to remind me. I know that I owe you, Renny. But I need this situation to die down. My marriage is on the line." For some reason that name Renny sounded so familiar to me, but I didn't know why. A few seconds later the call was over.

"Diamond, is everything okay? That conversation seemed pretty heated."

"I don't understand how my life went from a fairytale to a nightmare, almost overnight. And have you spoke to Blair. I've been trying to get in touch with her, but she's not answering."

"I don't know what's going on with Blair. I talked to her briefly, about a meeting I set up for her to be the new face for that makeup line. She didn't sound like herself at all."

"Really, do you think something is wrong?"

"My gut says yes, but I didn't want to pry."

"You not pry, that's a stretch."

"Listen, I learned my lesson from that Skee and Kirk situation. But honestly, rekindling her relationship with Kirk worked in our favor."

"How is that?"

"One of the executives saw a picture of Kirk and Blair together on the red carpet, at some movie premiere they attended recently. After that, Blair was an easy sell. They were practically salivating at the idea of not only having a beautiful up-and-coming actress, but one linked to a superstar basketball player like Kirk McKnight, to represent their new line."

"Wow, kudos to you for making that happen. I really am out the loop, though. I had no idea that Kirk and Blair were giving it another try."

"We're both out of the loop, because neither did I.

Blair mentioned they were going on a date, but I haven't heard anything else since. Maybe things didn't go well."

"That's too bad. After Michael, then Skee, Blair deserves to find a good guy."

"Honestly, I think it would be better if Blair was single for a while."

"Why?

"Relationships are a lot of work. In a lot of ways it's like job. Blair is trying to build a career. The last thing she needs is to get caught up in some man. Next thing, she'll be talking about weddings and babies. When you're trying to become the next Halle Berry, Kerry Washington, or Tyler Blake, you have to put those thoughts on the backburner."

"Sounds like you're speaking from personal experience."

"When I graduated from college and decided I wanted to be a successful business woman, I knew I would have to make some sacrifices. So, I chose a love life and you know what, I have no regrets."

"You don't think you can have it all?"

"No, but maybe you'll prove me wrong."

"If you're betting on me to prove you wrong, then you might come up short," Diamond giggled. "But I'll give it a try."

"The most important thing is that you're happy. I can honestly say, that without a man in my life and focusing on my career, I'm genuinely happy. But my choices might not work for everybody, and that's okay. I only hope that whatever choices Blair makes in her love life, she can live with it."

Blair

"Blair, it was a pleasure meeting with you. I think we can all agree you would be a perfect fit for our new makeup line. We'll be in touch."

"Thank you, so much, all of you," I smiled, before standing up and leaving. I was beaming inside when I left the meeting. Of course, Kennedy worked her magic and got the top executives to consider making me one of the faces of their new makeup line. If all went well, people would see my face plastered on billboards everywhere. I began daydreaming about that, while on the elevator. A noise, signaling the elevator doors were reopening, shook me out of my thoughts and I looked up.

"Blair, how are you?"

"I'm fine, and you?"

"I'm still one of the most sought after lawyers on the east coast, so I would say things are great."

"I see you're exactly the same, Michael. But as long as you're happy, that's all that matters."

"Speaking of being happy, how is that acting or modeling thing going for you?"

"Things are moving along. I actually just had a

meeting here that went very well."

"Well, at least something is working out for you."

"What is that supposed to mean?"

"You know, your boyfriend cheating on you for everybody to see. I'm sure it was difficult dealing with that sort of humiliation. So, since you can't seem to get it right in your personal life, I'm glad your professional one is going better. I would hate to think your life was completely pitiful, that's all."

"Save your pity, Michael. I'll be fine. I learned how to deal with cheating boyfriends from you, remember. At least Skee seems to have better taste in his sidepieces. I mean, Darcy is simply, well, you know," I smirked.

"So you know, I don't deal with Darcy anymore."

"Tell it to someone who cares. Who you're sleeping with is no longer a concern of mine. And who's in my bed shouldn't be a concern of yours, either. Now, excuse me, I have a life to go live," I scoffed, when the elevator finally came to a stop. The doors couldn't have opened fast enough, because occupying the same space as Michael was making my head hurt.

I exited out the building quickly, trying to keep as much distance as possible between Michael and me. Although I would never admit to him, my personal life was in complete disarray. I was once again trying my best to focus on my career, to escape the problems that seemed to follow me when it came to love. At the very moment love popped in my head, I heard my cell phone ringing and it was Kirk. I debated about whether or not to answer, but wanting to hear his voice won.

"Hi, how are you?"

"I would be a lot better if I could see you."

"I know, I want to see you, too, but I've been so busy. Kennedy has really been keeping the worked lined up for me lately."

'That's a beautiful thing, I'm happy for you, but you can't seem to squeeze anytime in there for me."

"Soon. I promise."

"How soon, Blair? It's already been weeks."

"I know. I do miss you, but luckily we talk often so that helps."

"I'm tired of talking to you over the phone. I want to hear your voice in person."

"Kirk, you will. That's Kennedy on the other line. I have to take it, but I'll call you later on." I wasn't even able to get out a bye before Kirk hung up on me. I switched over to Kennedy, wanting to get the Kirk situation out of my head. "Hey, what's up?"

"Girl, I got a call. They were very pleased with you!"

"They called already? I just left that meeting."

"That means they want you. I guarantee they'll be making an offer by the end of the week."

"I hope you're right. I need good news in my life."

"Is everything okay?"

"I don't know," I sighed.

"Listen, Diamond and I are about to head over to Empellon Cocina. You should come meet us."

"Some Mexican food does sound good."

"So, is that a yes?"

"Yep, I'm on the way."

"Cool, we'll see you shortly." After I hung up with

Kennedy, my phone began ringing again immediately and this time it was Skee. I sent his call straight to voicemail, before hailing a cab.

♥

"I'm so happy the three of us were able to get together. I really need you guys right now," Diamond huffed, before taking a sip of her mojito.

"Things haven't gotten any better with Cameron?"

"I'm afraid not. I think he might really be leaning towards getting a divorce. The very idea of that is about to send me postal."

"So, what are you going to do?"

"Ladies, I never thought I would be one of those pathetic women that would use a baby to hold onto a man, but now I understand what desperation drives you to."

"You're pregnant? I had no idea. I don't think you need to be drinking that mojito," Kennedy stated, reaching for Diamond's glass.

"I wish," Diamond said, pulling her drink from Kennedy's grasp. "I'm contemplating playing the pregnancy card in hopes of luring Cameron back in bed and making it a reality." Diamond glared at both Kennedy and I, waiting for our reaction. "I know. It's a horrible, disgusting idea, but I don't know what else to do."

"You have to keep the faith. You and Cameron are so in love. I believe you all are going to get through this stronger than ever."

"I hope you're right, Blair. Not only for my sake, but also Destiny. She really adores Cameron and with

Rico still in a coma, she has really turned to him as a father figure."

"Has Cameron still been spending time with her?"

"Thankfully, yes. He actually spends more time with Destiny than he does with me. It's probably because he can't stand being around me right now."

"I wish you would tell me what happened that pushed Cameron away."

Diamond and I looked at each other and then at Kennedy. I already knew most of Diamond's secrets, but she only recently confessed her role in Rico's shooting. I was completely blown away, but I also understood why she felt it had to be done. But Diamond was reluctant about coming clean with Kennedy. They were very close, but their friendship was somewhat different than the one Diamond and I shared. Neither of us was sure Kennedy would be so forgiving.

"I'm not ready to talk about it yet."

"If you say so. So Blair, do you want to discuss what has been bothering you lately?"

"Yeah, you haven't seemed like yourself. I've been so consumed with my own bullshit; I've totally been ignoring yours. Please, forgive me."

"All is forgiven, Diamond. I have to admit though, things are a little shaky for me."

"Do tell."

"Remember several weeks ago, I went out on a date with Kirk."

"Of course. I was ecstatic. Anything to get your mind off Skee."

"I had a great time with Kirk, even after Skee

confronted me in the bathroom."

"Skee confronted you in the bathroom...the nerve of that guy."

"Although he tried, he didn't ruin my evening with Kirk, because that night we had some of the greatest sex ever."

"Bitch, stop! You had sex with Kirk McKnight and you're just now sharing. Shame on you!" Diamond exclaimed.

"I know the sex was amazing. When I saw his body at that photo shoot, I wanted to get naked and throw myself at him. That's how hot he looked, bad attitude and all," Kennedy laughed.

"It was amazing. It was almost too perfect. I should've known, with my luck in the men department, it wasn't going to work out in my favor."

"What happened?"

"That morning when I woke up, Skee sent me a text. He apologized for how he acted the night before and wanted us to meet to get closure."

"Of course you agreed, because for some reason you have this weakness for Skee," Kennedy said, rolling her eyes.

"You're right, I agreed to meet him for lunch. We talked and everything seemed to be going fine, until I started feeling dizzy. Then, we left the restaurant and after that everything seems like a blur. Until I woke up a few hours later, in Skee's bed, naked. He said we had sex."

"And you don't remember having sex with him?"

"No. I did have a drink on an empty stomach. I

thought that's why I started feeling light headed."

"Being light headed and not remembering having sex is two totally different things. Are you sure Skee didn't spike your drink?"

"Kennedy, I think you might be reaching. It isn't like Skee hasn't had sex with Blair before. Why would he spike her drink to get her in bed?"

"Because he is a narcissistic asshole that wants everything his way. I'm sure he was beyond pissed after seeing Blair with Kirk. He probably figured that if he couldn't talk Blair into willingly having sex with him over lunch, then he would just take it. You know Skee feels entitled to take whatever he wants, anyway."

"Now that I think about it, my drink was already on the table when I arrived. Skee ordered a Bellini for me."

"If he did that shit to you, you should cut his dick off."

"Diamond, I completely agree with you," Kennedy said, slapping her hand.

"You all, this isn't funny."

"We're not laughing. I was dead ass serious. If this is true, Skee needs his balls handed to him, the audacity of that man. But I guess it's too late to get any blood work done, to find out. Do you think if you asked him, he would admit it?"

"Knowing how egotistical that motherfucker is, he just might."

"You all, I haven't told you the worst part yet."

"It gets worse? My goodness, Blair, what is it?" Kennedy questioned, as her and Diamond leaned forward to hear my response.

"I'm late."

"How late?"

"Two weeks and counting."

"Omigosh, you think you're pregnant, Blair?" Diamond blurted.

"Maybe your cycle is a little off this month," Kennedy said, in an attempt to make me feel better.

"I'm never off. I start like clockwork."

"Have you taken a pregnancy test?"

"Nope. I'm scared. I keep hoping that somehow, some way, Aunt Flo will come visit."

"You must be so stressed."

"Yes, I am! Plus, I didn't use protection with Kirk and I'm positive Skee didn't use a condom, because we never did, except for the very first time we had sex."

"Girl, chile cheese," Kennedy sighed, shaking her head.

"If you are pregnant, what are you going to do?"

"I don't know. That's the million dollar question."

Baller Bitches Volume 3

Coming Soon

A KING PRODUCTION

Dior Comes Home...

Rich
or
Famous
Part 2

JOY DEJA KING

Prologue

Lorenzo stepped out of his black Bugatti Coupe and entered the non-descript building in East Harlem. Normally, Lorenzo would have at least one henchman with him, but he wanted complete anonymity. When he made his entrance, the man Lorenzo planned on hiring was patiently waiting.

"I hope you came prepared for what I need."

"I wouldn't have wasted my time if I hadn't," Lorenzo stated before pulling out two pictures from a manila envelope and tossing them on the table.

"This is her?"

"Yes, her name is Alexus. Study this face very carefully, 'cause this is the woman you're going to bring to me, so I can kill."

"Are you sure you don't want me to handle it? Murder is included in my fee."

"I know, but personally killing this backstabbing snake is a gift to myself"

"Who is the other woman?"

"Her name is Lala."

"Do you want her dead, too?"

"I haven't decided. For now, just find her whereabouts and any other pertinent information. She also has a young daughter. I want you to find out how the little girl is doing. That will determine whether Lala lives or dies."

"Is there anybody else on your hit list?"

"This is it for now, but that might change at any moment. Now, get on your job, because I want results ASAP," Lorenzo demanded before tossing stacks of money next to the photos.

"I don't think there's a need to count. I'm sure it's all there," the hit man said, picking up one of the stacks and flipping through the bills.

"No doubt, and you can make even more, depending on how quickly I see results."

"I appreciate the extra incentive."

"It's not for you, it's for me. Everyone that is responsible for me losing the love of my life will pay in blood. The sooner the better."

Lorenzo didn't say another word and instead made his exit. He came and delivered; the rest was up to the hit man he had hired. But Lorenzo wasn't worried, he was just one of the many killers on his payroll hired to do the exact same job. He wanted to guarantee that Alexus was delivered to him alive. In his heart, he not only blamed Alexus and Lala for getting him locked up, but also held both of them responsible for Dior taking her own life. As he sat in his jail cell, Lorenzo promised himself that once he got out, if need be he would spend the rest of his life making sure both women received the ultimate retribution.

A KING PRODUCTION

*I'm Gettin' That
Helicopter Money...*

Bad
Bitch

JOY DEJA KING

"He need a Bad Bitch help him wit' cash flow.
I'm his Boss Bitch find me at his trap door.
I'm his type I'm what he asked for.
My nigga gettin' money,
I say get some more…"

Joy Deja King—Bad Bitch

Aaliyah

I came into the world surrounded by wealth and
privilege. I could've been anything I wanted to be
and I was…I was a Bad Bitch on my way to gettin'
that helicopter money and I was loving every minute of
it. I chose to walk on the same path as my Grandfather
and Father but in different shoes. As I thought about my
Grandfather, someone I respected and loved more than
just about anybody else in this world, there was one thing
I would do differently than him. If I had my way, Maya
would've been dead by now, but there was no doubt in
my mind that I would accomplish the very thing no one
had been able to do, including my Mother. I would make
sure Maya took her last breath and was six feet under,
sooner rather than later.

I stood in front of the arched window, soaking
in the breathtaking views of downtown Miami's skyline
from over 250 feet of open bay frontage. Watching as
the wind ushered the waves towards the shore, with the
sun's golden light shining on the rippling water was the

closest I had gotten to serenity in what seemed like many years. My life had me on a nonstop ride of one disaster after another. Starting with being accused of Sway's murder and then sitting in jail until I stood trial. Then my Grandfather being shot and in a coma, my parent's getting separated to breaking up with Amir which was still taking a toll on me emotionally after all these months. So many things in my life had changed, but so many other things stayed the same.

"Are you ready to go?"

"Dale, you startled me," I gasped, when I heard his voice. I turned around and he was standing in the door entrance.

"I apologize. Wherever your mind was, it had to be in deep thought."

"I guess you could say that."

"Is it anything you want to talk about?"

"No, I'm good."

"You sure? You know you can talk to me about anything. Remember you're my protégé. It's in my best interest to always make sure nothing is keeping you from being at the top of your game."

"I understand that but there's no need to worry. I won't disappoint you or myself. I'm in this game to win and I won't accept anything less than that."

"Then I take it you're ready for our meeting so lets go."

"Of course I am," I grinned, grabbing my purse off the living room table.

We headed outside towards the awaiting car and like always I looked up at the towering palm trees and a smile crept across my face. Miami had become a place that I treasured because everything about it gave me something that New York/New Jersey never could and that was peace.

"Do you feel prepared for the meeting?" Dale questioned, once again taking me away from my private thoughts. I knew he meant well but I was looking forward to having some much needed time alone.

"Yes. We've already gone over this. You're going to lead the conversation. I'm going to sit and listen and when you're ready for me to give additional critical information, you'll casually lean forward and that will be my cue to step in," I stated with an underlying annoyance in my tone.

"No need to get irritated," Dale said, placing his hand on my upper left thigh. "You don't seem quite yourself today so you can't blame me for being concerned. You know how important this meeting is."

"I get that, but have I ever dropped the ball on anything that has to do with business?"

"No and I wanna make sure you keep it that way."

I turned and gazed out the backseat window as the driver made his way to Indian Creek Island for our meeting. I didn't respond to what Dale said because I couldn't deny that I was "off" today. As much stress as the East Coast brought me it was home and I missed my family and more importantly my heart ached for Amir.

"Is it Maya, is that what has your mind someplace else?"

I simply nodded my head yes. I figured that sounded much better than having to confess to Dale I was yearning for my ex.

"I already told you when the time was right Maya would be handled. You need to let that go for now. We have much bigger and significant deals on the table right now that have to be dealt with."

"You're right. I just don't want Maya to slip away. She's been a thorn in my family's lives for far too long and the Peaches situation was the final nail in her coffin. Even the thought of her slipping through my fingers, burns me up inside."

"That's not gonna happen. I got my people keeping track of all her movements. Like I promised you, when the time is right, I will bring Maya to you and you can personally take pleasure in ending her life once and for all. You have to believe that."

"I do. I do believe that," I nodded, looking back out the window. I had learned never to doubt Dale's word. Each thing that he promised me thus far, he delivered it and more. Proof of that was being shown to me once again, as the driver made his way up the long elegant landscaped driveway at 12 Indian Creek Drive. This home was located on Dade County's most prestigious Private Island. I'm talking homes that start at 30 million and go nowhere but up. Juan Alvarez, the head of one of the most profitable and deadliest Mexican Cartels, owned the palatial estate we were now entering. This was the man that would take me to making that helicopter money, purchasing private jets, buying islands and shit like that.

After our ordeal with Peaches and I had to murder that bitch, I became completed fixated on two things: Killing Maya and making money. Dale promised that he would make sure I achieved both. When I realized Maya had set me up to be killed, she was at the top of my list to fall. Dale convinced me to hold back and let that shit settle for a while. At first I resisted his suggestion but I had watched Dale and I respected how he moved in handling his business so I listened to his logic and followed it. He told me to focus my energy on stacking paper because the money would give me all the power I needed, to eliminate Maya and just about anybody else I felt was a threat to me or my family.

After several months of soaking up any and every business move Dale and his brother Emory made, I became the female version of them which made me all the more lethal. I became meticulous with how I handled money, drugs and people we did business with and the more moves I made I wanted to make even bigger ones. Because men dominated the drug business, I had no problem using the female persuasion to my advantage. I dangled it just enough to keep my creditability intact but to also allow our business associates to lower their wall enough for me to get the information I needed to close better deals. It was that calculated maneuvering that put the name Juan Alvarez on my radar. Everyone including

Emory swore it would be impossible to get to him. The only person that didn't flinch was Dale. Like me he loved a challenge and like he promised, against all the odds here we were.

When we pulled through the iron gates in every direction you turned there appeared to be armed guards. He had an army watching over him like he was the President of the United States but in the world of drugs I guess you could say Juan Alvarez was.

"This place is unbelievable," I commented, as we got closer to his massive mansion. I had lived and seen many stunning homes in my short lifetime but this place was something completely different. The sprawling European design was beyond breathtaking.

"That it is. But if we play our cards right we'll be able to have one just like it," Dale stated, with unwavering confidence. I couldn't help but smile because like always he made me a believer.

In the brief moment from me glancing over at Dale and smiling at his comment, before our driver could even step out and open the door for us, there was an armed guard on both sides of the car doing that job for him. They immediately began patting us down and I looked over at Dale and he nodded his head letting me know to go with the flow. I planned on doing that anyway. We had come this far I wasn't about to fuck it up now.

"Follow us," the guard that had just finished patting Dale down said, directing us towards the front entrance. A 40 ft. hand-painted ceiling with gold leaf accents in the foyer greeted us. I wanted to gasp as we walked through what had to be over 40,000 square ft. of what I would describe as a grand and majestic masterpiece. After what felt like a never-ending marathon we finally ended up outside. Off in the distance I noticed the dock with a huge yacht and a private lagoon. But it was the over 50-foot long mosaic tiled 24k gold lined pool that truly had me in awe. The water seemed to be calling my name but that feeling didn't last long because once again there were armed guards posted everywhere. Seeing them took all sense of peace or relaxation away but I assumed that was the purpose they were there to serve.

"Mr. Alvarez, your guest have arrived," the guard that had led us in announced. I still couldn't see him because he was sitting down on a high gloss white circular sofa with his back turned to us. I noticed him signaling the guard by putting up one finger. "He's on a call. He'll be with you both shortly," the guard informed us.

I appreciated having a little extra time before we were formally introduced because out of nowhere a burst of nervousness crept up on me. That was so not my style as Dale had taught me how to remain calm even under the most strenuous situations. He warned me that keeping a composed demeanor could be the difference between living and dying in certain predicaments. I quickly closed my eyes and let out a soft breath to center myself and regain control. In that instant I realized where all the anxiety was coming from. I was about to meet the man that would change my life forever.

A King Production presents...

A Novel

JOY DEJA KING

Power

NO ONE MAN SHOULD HAVE ALL THAT POWER...BUT THERE WERE TWO

JOY DEJA KING

Chapter 1

Underground King

Alex stepped into his attorney's office to discuss what was always his number one priority…business. When he sat down their eyes locked and there was complete silence for the first few seconds. This was Alex's way of setting the tone of the meeting. His silence spoke volumes. This might've been his attorney's office but he was the head nigga in charge and nothing got started until he decided it was time to speak. Alex felt this approach was necessary. You see, after all these years of them doing business, attorney George Lofton still wasn't used to dealing with a man like Alex; a dirt-poor kid who could've easily died in the projects he was born in, but instead made millions. It wasn't done the ski mask way but it was still illegal.

They'd first met when Alex was a sixteen-year-old kid growing up in TechWood Homes, a housing project in Atlanta. Alex and his best friend, Deion, had been arrested because the principal found 32 crack vials in

Alex's book bag. Another kid had tipped the principal off and the principal subsequently called the police. Alex and Deion were arrested and suspended from school. His mother called George, who had the charges against them dismissed and they were allowed to go back to school. But that wasn't the last time he would use George. He was arrested at twenty-two for attempted murder and for trafficking cocaine a year later. Alex was acquitted on both charges. George Lofton later became known as the best trial attorney in Atlanta, but Alex had also become the best at what he did. And since it was Alex's money that kept Mr. Lofton in designer suits, million dollar homes and foreign cars, he believed he called the shots, and dared his attorney to tell him differently.

Alex noticed that what seemed like a long period of silence made Mr. Lofton feel uncomfortable, which he liked. Out of habit, in order to camouflage the discomfort, his attorney always kept bottled water within arm's reach. He would cough then take a swig, lean back in his chair, raise his eyebrows a little, trying to give a look of certainty, though he wasn't completely confident at all in Alex's presence. The reason was because Alex did what many had thought would be impossible, especially men like George Lofton. He had gone from a knucklehead, low-level drug dealer to an underground king and an unstoppable respected criminal boss.

Before finally speaking, Alex gave an intense stare into George Lofton's piercing eyes. They were not only the bluest he had ever seen, but also some of the most calculating. The latter is what Alex found so compelling. A calculating attorney working on his behalf could almost guarantee a get out of jail card for the duration of his criminal career.

"Have you thought over what we briefly discussed the other day?" Alex asked his attorney, finally breaking the silence.

"Yes I have, but I want to make sure I understand you correctly. You want to give me six hundred thousand to represent you or your friend Deion if you are ever arrested and have to stand trial again in the future?"

Alex assumed he had already made himself clear based on their previous conversations and was annoyed by what he now considered a repetitive question. "George, you know I don't like repeating myself. That's exactly what I'm saying. Are we clear?"

"So this is an unofficial retainer."

"Yes, you can call it that."

George stood and closed the blinds then walked over to the door that led to the reception area. He turned the deadbolt so they wouldn't be disturbed. George sat back behind the desk. "You know that if you and your friend Deion are ever on the same case that I can't represent the both of you."

"I know that."

"So what do you propose I do if that was ever to happen?"

"You would get him the next best attorney in Atlanta," Alex said without hesitation. Deion was Alex's best friend—had been since the first grade. They were now business partners, but the core of their bond was built on that friendship, and because of that Alex would always look out for Deion's best interest.

"That's all I need to know."

Alex clasped his hands and stared at the ceiling for a moment thinking that maybe it was a bad idea bringing the money to George. Maybe he should have just put it somewhere safe only known to him and his mom. He quickly dismissed his concerns.

"Okay. Where's the money?" Alex presented him with two leather briefcases. George opened the first one and was glad to see that it was all hundred-dollar bills. When he closed the briefcase he asked, "There is no need to count this is there?"

"You can count it if you want, but it's all there."

George took another swig of water. The cash made him nervous. He planned to take it directly to one of his bank safe deposit boxes. The two men stood. Alex was a foot taller than George; he had flawless mahogany skin, a deep brown with a bit of a red tint, broad shoulders, very large hands, and a goatee. He was a man's man. With such a powerful physical appearance, Alex kept his style very low-key. His only display of wealth was a pricey diamond watch that his best friend and partner Deion had bought him for his birthday.

"I'll take good care of this, and you," his attorney said, extending his hand to Alex.

"With this type of money, I know you will," Alex

stated without flinching. Alex gave one last lingering stare into his attorney's piercing eyes. "We do have a clear understanding…correct?"

"Of course. I've never let you down and I never will. That, I promise you." The men shook hands and Alex made his exit with the same coolness as his entrance.

With Alex embarking on a new, potentially dangerous business venture, he wanted to make sure that he had all his bases covered. The higher up he seemed to go on the totem pole, the costlier his problems became. But Alex welcomed new challenges because he had no intentions of ever being a nickel and dime nigga again.

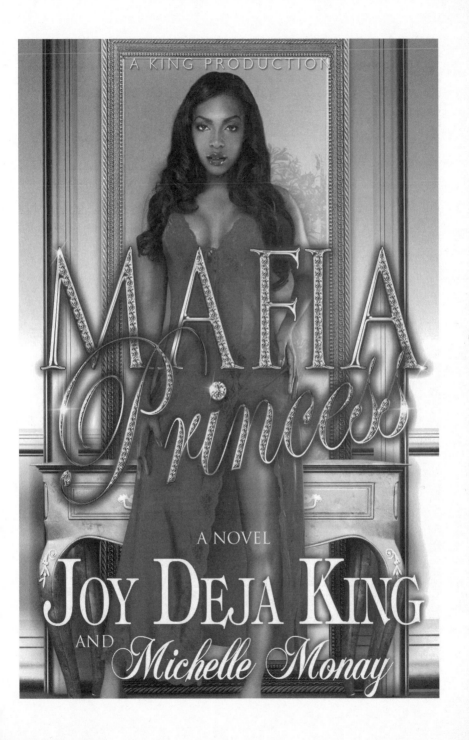

A KING PRODUCTION

MAFIA
Princess

A NOVEL

JOY DEJA KING
AND *Michelle Monay*

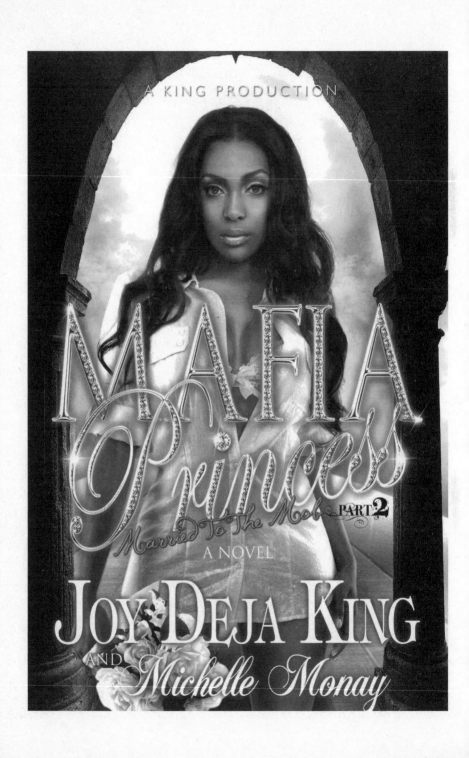

A KING PRODUCTION

MAFIA
Princess
PART 2
Married To The Mob

A NOVEL

JOY DEJA KING
AND Michelle Monay

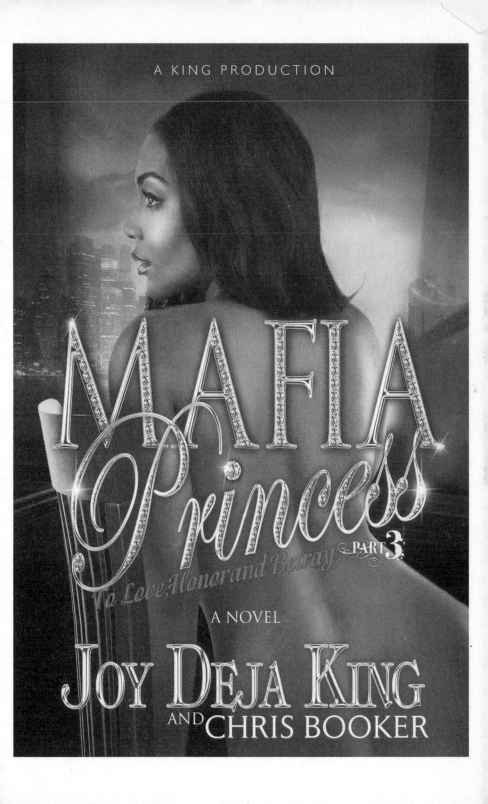

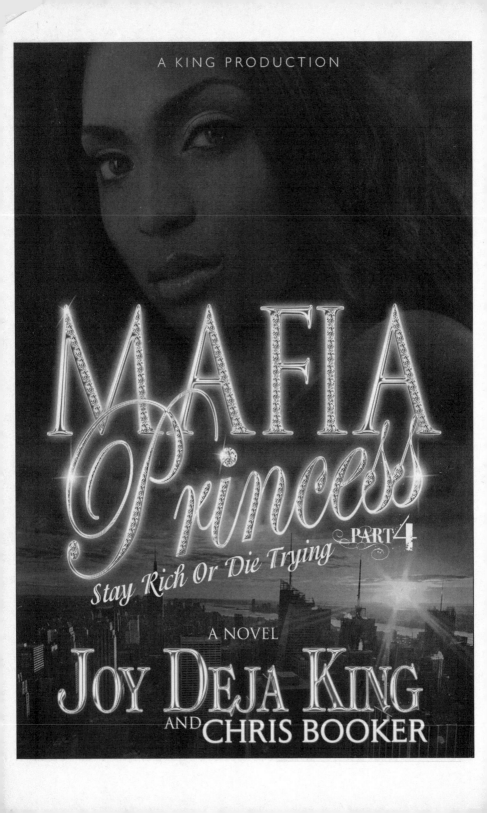

A KING PRODUCTION

Young Diamond Books
PRESENTS

A young adult urban tale

Ride Wit' Me 2

JOY DEJA KING

Coming Soon!

Genesis & Genevieve...Born Sinners

A King A King Production Order Form

A King Production
P.O. Box 912
Collierville, TN 38027
www.joydejaking.com
www.twitter.com/joydejaking

Name: _____

Address: _____

City/State: _____

Zip: _____

QUANTITY	TITLES	PRICE	TOTAL
____	Bitch	$15.00	____
____	Bitch Reloaded	$15.00	____
____	The Bitch Is Back	$15.00	____
____	Queen Bitch	$15.00	____
____	Last Bitch Standing	$15.00	____
____	Superstar	$15.00	____
____	Ride Wit' Me	$12.00	____
____	Stackin' Paper	$15.00	____
____	Trife Life To Lavish	$15.00	____
____	Trife Life To Lavish II	$15.00	____
____	Stackin' Paper II	$15.00	____
____	Rich or Famous	$15.00	____
____	Bitch A New Beginning	$15.00	____
____	Mafia Princess Part 1	$15.00	____
____	Mafia Princess Part 2	$15.00	____
____	Mafia Princess Part 3	$15.00	____
____	Mafia Princess Part 4	$15.00	____
____	Boss Bitch	$15.00	____
____	Baller Bitches Vol. 1	$15.00	____
____	Baller Bitches Vol. 2	$15.00	____
____	Bad Bitch	$15.00	____
____	Princess Fever "Birthday Bash"	$9.99	____

Shipping/Handling (Via Priority Mail) $6.50 1-2 Books, $8.95 3-4 Books add $1.95 for ea. Additional book.

Total: $_____ **FORMS OF ACCEPTED PAYMENTS:** Certified or government issued checks and money Orders, all mail in orders take 5-7 Business days to be delivered.

A King Production
Order Form

A King Production
P.O. Box 912
Collierville, TN 38027
www.joydejaking.com
www.twitter.com/joydejaking

Name: _____

Address: _____

City/State: _____

Zip: _____

QUANTITY	TITLES	PRICE	TOTAL
____	Bitch	$15.00	____
____	Bitch Reloaded	$15.00	____
____	The Bitch Is Back	$15.00	____
____	Queen Bitch	$15.00	____
____	Last Bitch Standing	$15.00	____
____	Superstar	$15.00	____
____	Ride Wit' Me	$12.00	____
____	Stackin' Paper	$15.00	____
____	Trife Life To Lavish	$15.00	____
____	Trife Life To Lavish II	$15.00	____
____	Stackin' Paper II	$15.00	____
____	Rich or Famous	$15.00	____
____	Bitch A New Beginning	$15.00	____
____	Mafia Princess Part 1	$15.00	____
____	Mafia Princess Part 2	$15.00	____
____	Mafia Princess Part 3	$15.00	____
____	Mafia Princess Part 4	$15.00	____
____	Boss Bitch	$15.00	____
____	Baller Bitches Vol. 1	$15.00	____
____	Baller Bitches Vol. 2	$15.00	____
____	Bad Bitch	$15.00	____
____	Princess Fever "Birthday Bash"	$9.99	____

Shipping/Handling (Via Priority Mail) $6.50 1-2 Books, $8.95 3-4 Books add $1.95 for ea. Additional book.

Total: $_____ FORMS OF ACCEPTED PAYMENTS: Certified or government issued checks and money Orders, all mail in orders take 5-7 Business days to be delivered.